"Stop! Police!"

The woman revved the engine and took off, the back end of the sedan swerving a bit as she fought to gain control. Danica peered at the license plate only to find it was covered in mud.

"Come, Hutch."

Her partner wheeled toward her and loped back to her side. She glanced over to where Luke was bent over Caden. "Is he okay?"

"I think so." His words were muffled, and she realized he had the baby cradled in his arms, his face buried against the little boy's head.

Using her hands-free function, she called the local police to put out an alert for a black sedan with muddy license plates.

"The driver tried to kidnap a baby in a stroller."

* * *

Pacific Northwest K-9 Unit

Laura Scott has always loved romance and read faith-based books by Grace Livingston Hill in her teenage years. She's thrilled to have been given the opportunity to retire from thirty-eight years of nursing to become a full-time author. Laura has published over thirty books for Love Inspired Suspense. She has two adult children and lives in Milwaukee, Wisconsin, with her husband of thirty-five years. Please visit Laura at laurascottbooks.com, as she loves to hear from her readers.

Books by Laura Scott

Love Inspired Suspense

Hiding in Plain Sight
Amish Holiday Vendetta

Justice Seekers

Soldier's Christmas Secrets
Guarded by the Soldier
Wyoming Mountain Escape
Hiding His Holiday Witness
Rocky Mountain Standoff
Fugitive Hunt

Rocky Mountain K-9 Unit

Hiding in Montana

Pacific Northwest K-9 Unit

Shielding the Baby

Visit the Author Profile page at LoveInspired.com for more titles.

SHIELDING
THE BABY

LAURA SCOTT

❧
LOVE INSPIRED SUSPENSE
INSPIRATIONAL ROMANCE

Special thanks and acknowledgment are given to Laura Scott for her contribution to the Pacific Northwest K-9 Unit miniseries.

LOVE INSPIRED® SUSPENSE

INSPIRATIONAL ROMANCE

Recycling programs for this product may not exist in your area.

ISBN-13: 978-1-335-58762-6

Shielding the Baby

Copyright © 2023 by Harlequin Enterprises ULC

For questions and comments about the quality of this book, please contact us at CustomerService@Harlequin.com.

Love Inspired
22 Adelaide St. West, 41st Floor
Toronto, Ontario M5H 4E3, Canada
www.LoveInspired.com

Printed in U.S.A.

The Lord thy God in the midst of thee is mighty;
he will save, he will rejoice over thee with joy;
he will rest in his love, he will joy over thee with singing.
—*Zephaniah* 3:17

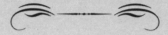

This book is dedicated to the brave men and women who work for our national park service. Without them, we wouldn't be able to enjoy the beauty of wildlife and nature.

ONE

"**S**hots fired. Two victims near the Longmire Suspension Bridge. PNK9 response requested." The dispatcher's voice came through Pacific Northwest K-9 officer Danica Hayes's radio. She was in the Mount Rainier National Park with her K-9 partner, Hutch, accompanied by her colleague Colt Maxwell and his K-9, Sampson.

"Colt and I are on it." She disconnected from the call. "Let's go. But we'll need to take the SUVs— the bridge is five miles from here."

"Race you," Colt said with a cheeky smile.

They'd been about to leave the park after successfully apprehending the man responsible for assaulting a hiker. She jogged to her SUV, quickly putting her male German shepherd in the back crate area. Sliding behind the wheel, she made a sharp U-turn toward the Longmire Suspension Bridge. Colt was hot on her heels in his SUV.

Why hadn't they heard the shots? Five miles wasn't that far, and out here the sound would carry, especially in mid-April, when the park wasn't busy. She frowned, pulled over, then quickly retrieved Hutch.

Shielding the Baby

From here she could see two people lying on the ground not far from the bridge entryway. Before Colt and Sampson could cross over to join her, more gunfire echoed, louder this time.

"Take cover!" Colt shouted.

Danica lunged toward the thick cluster of trees, Hutch at her side. Colt went in the opposite direction. She dropped to her knees in the brush, her arm protectively around Hutch's neck, scanning the area. There was nothing up ahead, so she turned around. A flash of movement caught her eye. She narrowed her gaze as a woman with dark hair and wearing a dark blue parka moved through the trees. The woman glanced furtively over her shoulder. Their gazes clashed, and the flash of recognition was unmistakable.

The woman was Mara Gilmore, the PNK9's newest crime scene investigator. For a moment, Danica was confused. How had Mara gotten here so quickly? Then she realized Mara wasn't working today. Dropping her gaze to Mara's hands, she half expected to see a gun, but the tech had already disappeared through the brush.

She blinked, momentarily frozen. What was Mara doing here? Was she running away from the shooter? Had she seen something? Mara's expression flashed in her mind. Guilt? Fear? A combination of both? Either way, she needed to find the team's tech, to discover what, if anything, she might know. She jumped out from the trees. "I'm going after a witness," she called to Colt. "Let's go, Hutch!"

Hutch immediately bounded forward, anxious to be on the move. "No, Hutch, this way." Danica used his leash to correct his path so that he was following Mara. Danica ran with her ninety-pound black-and-tan partner, her gaze searching for Mara. The more she thought about it, the less likely it seemed that Mara was involved in the shooting. The look on her face must have been fear. Still, she wanted to reassure the newest member of their team there was no reason to be afraid.

Shame on her for thinking the worst. Blame it on her tumultuous childhood.

Hutch slowed down, sniffing the ground, then lifting his snout to the air as if trying to capture Mara's scent. It wasn't easy, as she hadn't provided him with a specific scent to find. Yet she trusted Hutch to do his best.

Her K-9 shifted, heading off at a diagonal direction from the area where she'd seen Mara. Keeping pace with her partner wasn't easy; her feet slipped on the areas of snow and ice.

They covered roughly two miles before Hutch stopped, sniffing along the side of the road. The same road she and Colt had come up just fifteen minutes ago. Her K-9 sat and looked up at her, signaling this was the end of the trail.

"Good boy, Hutch." She lavishly praised her partner, pulling the tattered bunny from her coat pocket. She tossed it to him. He caught it midair and pranced around like he was king of the world. Normally the routine made her smile.

Not today.

Mara must have left the park in a vehicle she'd parked nearby. The time it had taken her and Hutch to get here made it unlikely they'd be able to find her. The good news was, Mara hadn't been lost. The tech had found her way to the road. Yet it was still strange that Mara had run away rather than sticking around to offer her statement.

Blowing out a frustrated breath, she called Hutch over, took his bunny and headed back down the road to the bridge.

Colt, tall and blond, and his bloodhound K-9 Sampson were there, examining the two bodies. He looked at her when she approached. "One male and one female victim, both in their late twenties, and both shot in the back."

"I saw Mara Gilmore running from the scene. It's possible she may have witnessed something and took off in fear."

"I saw Mara, too," Colt agreed with a frown. "It's odd she was here. And that she left the scene."

She stared down at the two bodies for a moment. "We need to alert the chief." Chief Donovan Fanelli was their boss, and he'd want to know that one of their own was a possible witness.

"I already called him." Colt grimaced. "I don't want to jump to conclusions, but I thought it was strange how Mara ran off like that. I figured Hutch would have a better chance of tracking her, so I stayed here with the bodies."

"I don't want to jump to conclusions, either, but I know she saw and recognized me." Danica managed a wry smile. "She's a tech, not a cop. Being in the line of fire must have scared her. Hopefully she'll return very soon to let us know what she saw."

Colt rose to his feet. "I hope so. By the way, the National Park Service crime scene techs are on their way back."

It made sense that he'd stayed with the bodies, as Sampson's specialty was cadaver recovery. "What's going on, Colt?" She stared at the two victims. "Why would anyone kill them?"

Before he could respond, the crime scene van pulled up on beside their SUVs. Danica and Colt stepped back to give them access to the bodies. They watched as the techs went to work.

"We have an ID here on both vics." Trent Ward, the taller park ranger tech, looked over at them. "Male is Jonas Digby and female is Stacey Stark."

The names didn't ring any bells for her. At Colt's shrug, she assumed the same was true for him.

Overhead, a yellow-and-black chopper came in flying low. Shielding her eyes from the sun, she watched it descend. "Is that the chief?"

"Yes. He's bringing Willow Bates, too. They were both at headquarters when I called."

Their PNK9 headquarters located in Olympia, Washington, was roughly a ninety-minute drive from Mount Rainier. She watched as the chopper set down in a large open field not far from the bridge. Donovan and Willow both jumped out, along with Willow's K-9, a German short-haired pointer named Star. Their chief was tall, with broad shoulders, salt-and-pepper hair, and piercing blue eyes. He strode purposefully toward them, Willow and Star trailing behind him.

Minutes later, they were huddled together near the crime scene. "We heard that a witness reported a woman with dark hair wearing a navy blue parka shot the vics," Willow said.

What? Danica swallowed hard, the similarities too much to ignore. "I saw Mara Gilmore wearing a dark blue parka and running from the scene." Danica met Donovan's serious gaze. "I know she saw me, too. Hutch and I tried to catch up to her—we assumed she was afraid of the gunfire—but we lost her near the road."

Their boss grimaced. "I don't like this. I wouldn't want anyone from our team to be considered a possible suspect. Although the description is vague. Lots of people have blue parkas and dark hair."

"I didn't see her with a gun," Danica quickly pointed out.

"And neither of us saw her shooting," Colt added.

"I'll call Mara." Donovan lifted his phone to his ear. After several long moments, he grimaced and shoved it back in his pocket. "No answer. The call went straight to voice mail."

That didn't make any sense. Why wouldn't Mara talk to their boss?

"What do you know so far?" Donovan asked.

"Colt and I didn't hear the original gunfire, although there were additional shots fired once we arrived on scene. It's possible the killer used a silencer with the first shots." Danica waved a hand. "It would sure help to interview that witness. I find it strange that we didn't see anyone other than Mara, and we've been in this general area of the park for a couple of hours. The only thing I can come up with is that the shooter had a vehicle stashed nearby."

Willow had gone over to check on the victims. Her gaze was somber when she returned. "Look, I know Mara pretty well—we've gotten close since she joined the team. The male vic, Jonas Digby? He's Mara's former boyfriend. And the woman, Stacey Stark, is Digby's new girlfriend. I know it looks bad, especially because the witness's description matches Mara as the shooter, but I know she couldn't have done this. Mara isn't a killer."

"Yeah, right," Trent muttered from behind them as he removed something from the van. "Protecting your own as usual."

Chief Donovan's face reddened at the accusation. Danica didn't want to believe Mara was guilty, yet the crime scene tech certainly hadn't come forward proclaiming her innocence, either.

"Let's get somewhere private." Donovan gestured for the team to step farther away from the scene.

"The Longmire welcome center isn't far," Colt said. "We can go there for warmth and privacy."

"Officers?" A female crime scene tech rushed over. "I thought you'd want to see this. We found it in the snow near the two victims."

She held up a plastic evidence bag containing a thin gold bracelet, a charm engraved with the letter *M*.

Willow gasped. "That's Mara's bracelet. Her father gave it to her for her sixteenth birthday."

Donovan's expression turned even more grim. "Thanks for letting us know," he told the crime scene tech. The woman nodded, then hurried back to place the evidence in the van.

No one said anything for a long moment. Donovan's expression was grave. "If Mara is a suspect, we'll need to make sure to have all evidence handled by the park ranger crime scene techs to avoid any conflict of interest." Donovan turned to Colt. "You mentioned the visitor center?"

"Yeah, let's go. You can ride with me, Chief." Normally Colt liked to crack jokes, but the somber situation put a damper on the normal camaraderie the team shared.

"Willow, why don't you ride with me?" Danica said. "Star can take the back seat."

"Okay," Willow agreed. As soon as they were settled in the SUV, she added, "I'm telling you, Danica, Mara didn't do this."

Danica glanced at her. "I know it's hard to believe, Willow. And I honestly didn't see her shoot anyone, or even have a gun. What bothers me is that she didn't come forward when she recognized me. Even if she was afraid and hiding, wouldn't she answer Donovan's call?"

Willow closed her eyes for a moment. "There has to be a good reason. Something more going on than we know."

"Like what? And why was Mara here at Mount Rainier, where her ex-boyfriend was with his new girl-friend?"

Willow shook her head grimly. "I wish I knew."

The trip to the welcome center didn't take long. Soon they were huddled inside the center, which was thank-fully empty of visitors.

"Thanks for meeting me here." Donovan brought the impromptu meeting to order. "I wish the entire team could participate, but we'll have to make do."

The Pacific Northwest K-9 Unit had been founded ten years ago, primarily funded through a generous fed-eral grant bankrolled by Roland Evans, a philanthropist who strongly believed in their core mission of solving the most difficult crimes that transpired throughout sev-eral police jurisdictions in Washington State, including the three national parks. Danica was proud to be one of twelve federal law enforcement K-9 officers reporting to Chief Donovan Fanelli. Their team also had two dedicated crime scene techs, Mara Gilmore and Bartholomew Davis. With Mara as a potential suspect, Bart wouldn't be allowed anywhere near the case, either. And really, thinking about the team made Danica realize that Mara's half brother, PNK9 officer Asher Gilmore, might need to keep his distance, too.

She glanced at her fellow officers, Colt and Willow. They had investigated many difficult cases, but she sensed this would be their toughest yet.

"We need intel." Donovan pulled out his phone. "Jasmin must have something by now."

Jasmin Eastwood was the PNK9 team's technical expert and always ready to assist.

Donovan placed the call on speaker so they could all hear. "Jasmin? What do you have on the witness who reported seeing a dark-haired woman shoot the victims?"

"Chief, the call came in via a burner phone," Jasmin informed them. "What I found interesting is that the caller's voice was distorted by a mechanical device. I listened twice, and honestly can't say if the caller was a man or woman. Because it was a burner phone, there's no way to get a trace."

Donovan's brow furrowed as he digested this information. Already the puzzle pieces didn't fit. In Danica's experience, an untraceable witness was very suspicious. Was it possible the mechanical-voice witness was really the killer?

"We have two victims, Jonas Digby and Stacey Stark," Donovan said. "Run their names through the system."

There was a brief silence as Jasmin did the search. Each team member's face was grim as they waited.

"Chief? No criminal records for either vic. Stacey Stark is from Ashford, which is only a few miles from where you are now. She owns three luxe yet charmingly rustic Stark Lodges, each near a national park, with a business partner, Eli Ballard. One of their properties is between Rainier and the small town of Ashford. That's her last known address. The other two lodges are located near the other National Parks, Olympic and North Cascades."

"We need info on Eli Ballard, her business partner. What about the vics' families?" Donovan asked.

"Digby is an only child, parents deceased. Stacey's brother, Luke Stark, lives at the Stark Lodge near Mount Rainier. He may have motive, as he's the only family member Stacey has and logically stands to inherit the properties now that she's gone."

"That's motive, and his location being near the park provides opportunity," Willow said eagerly.

Danica didn't mention that Mara had the similar motive and opportunity, as she'd been here at the crime scene. Willow's dedication to Mara was admirable, but the rookie CSI had only been with them for a few months. What did they really know about her? Had Mara snapped after the breakup with her boyfriend?

"We'll investigate all angles," Donovan said, caution underlying his tone. "We must keep an open mind on any and all possibilities."

Danica nodded, as did Colt and Willow.

"Anything else, Jasmin?" Donovan asked.

"Not yet, but I'll keep digging."

"Thanks." Donovan cleared his throat. "You should all know, that from this point forward all evidence must be handled by the National Park Service to preserve the integrity of the investigation. However, we will continue to work the case. Danica, I'd like you to talk to Luke Stark. Give him the news of his sister's death and ask where he's been during the time frame of the murders. I'll look into Digby's background. We'll also need to search both victims' living quarters for clues. If there's anything resembling evidence, make sure to call in a park service crime scene tech."

"I'm on it," Danica said.

"Colt, when Jasmin has info on Eli Ballard, I'd like you to interview him."

"Will do," Colt agreed.

Donovan gave a terse nod. "Stay in touch."

Danica stepped back from the group. "Come, Hutch." She was anxious to talk to Luke Stark.

As much as she didn't want one of their own to be complicit in this crime, Danica was determined to uncover the truth.

No matter what.

Jiggling his nine-month old son, Caden, on his hip, Luke Stark tried to tidy the kitchen. The baby was being unusually clingy.

Or maybe this was normal. What did he know? He was still fumbling through this whole being-a-dad thing. Having a baby hadn't been part of the plan, and now that his wife, Annette, was dead, he was all the kid had.

He loved Caden, more than he'd thought was possible to love anyone. But that alone didn't make this situation easy.

"We'll figure it out together, right, kiddo?"

Caden babbled something incomprehensible and grabbed Luke's nose, making him laugh.

"Does that mean you're ready to sit down for a bit?" Luke bent to set Caden on the floor, but the little boy began to cry.

"Okay, okay." He lifted him back up into his arms. The dishes could wait until Caden fell asleep.

A knock at the door made him frown. The hour was going on seven thirty, the sun making its descent behind the horizon. Shifting Caden to his other hip, he went over to peer through the peephole.

A blond-haired woman wearing a light green uniform covered in a dark green winter jacket stood there. The jacket was open, giving him a glimpse of the patch above her left pocket embroidered with *PNK9 Unit.*

Cautiously, he opened the door to greet her. The K-9 part registered when he took note of the large black-and-tan German shepherd wearing a black K-9 vest sitting beside her. "Ah, can I help you?"

"Luke Stark?"

"Yes." He still didn't understand, even after the pretty blonde flashed a badge. "Is something wrong? Did one of the lodge guests report a crime?"

"I'm Officer Danica Hayes, and this is my K-9 partner, Hutch." She lowered her badge. "May we come in?"

His army medic instincts went on full alert. He'd been on enough battlefields to know when something was wrong, but he couldn't imagine what had brought the K-9 cop to his door. "Yes, of course."

"Doggy." Caden said the word clear as day, which was disconcerting, as his son hadn't mastered *daddy.* The little boy leaned forward, extending his hand toward the K-9.

"No, Caden." The warning came out sharper than intended. "He's not a pet."

Officer Hayes stepped inside, then put a hand on the German shepherd's head. "Friend, Hutch." She rested her hand on his arm, making it tingle, then repeated the gesture with Caden. "Friends."

The shepherd sniffed at them for long moments before his tail wagged.

"Mr. Stark," she began.

"Call me Luke." He gestured for her to come farther into the room, while keeping his distance. Not because of the dog, but the weird reaction elicited by her touch. "Have a seat."

She seemed a bit uncomfortable but did as he asked. When they were both seated, she met his gaze directly. "I'm afraid I have some bad news. Your sister, Stacey, is dead."

His jaw dropped in shock. "What? How? Why? What happened?"

"She was found in Mount Rainier National Park, near the Longmire Suspension Bridge." The K-9 officer's light brown eyes bored into his. "Do you know why your sister went there?"

"I—no. I don't." For a moment he was transported back to three months earlier, when he'd been notified that Annette had died. Leaving him an unexpectedly single father. A wave of grief hit hard, and he struggled to hold it together. "D-did she fall off the bridge?"

The light brown eyes continued to hold his. "I'm sorry, Luke, but I need to ask where you were between five and five thirty this evening."

It took a moment for him to understand what this was about. Pushing aside his sorrow, he straightened in his seat. There was no mistaking the fact she considered him a possible suspect. "I was in the kitchen with Vera, the lodge cook. She was helping me with Caden—he's teething."

"You were with Vera the whole time?" she pressed. "I'll need her last name and to talk to her to verify that."

"Yeah, I was with her the whole time. Vera Johnson. She put a water ring thingy in the freezer so Caden could gnaw on it. Then she gave me a book to read him." His mind whirled as he pulled the boy farther into his lap, to stop him from leaning over to pet the dog. "I stayed in the kitchen, because it was close to dinnertime anyway."

"When can I speak with her?"

"I'm pretty sure she's gone for the day by now, but she'll be back in the morning." He narrowed his gaze. "Based on your questions, you must believe Stacey was murdered."

His blunt statement seemed to catch the female officer off guard. After spending the past ten years in the army, he wasn't accustomed to sugarcoating the truth.

Instead of responding, she took a moment to look around his suite. The area was spacious, yet cozy, with an amazing view of Mount Rainier from his balcony. It wasn't hard to guess what she was thinking, and he bit back a flash of anger.

"Yes, this is a nice place, but I also pay rent to live here with Caden." He didn't mince words. "I had no reason to hurt Stacey, especially now that we've been reconnecting after my discharge from the army. I'm not sure why she was in the park, but that doesn't seem unusual. It's so close by."

Officer Hayes's gaze returned to his. "Army? For how long?"

"Yes, medic for ten years." He didn't elaborate.

"Do you know a man by the name of Jonas Digby?"

"Um…" He searched his memory. His days and nights had been centered around his son. "The name is familiar, yes. Stacey mentioned they'd started seeing each other, but I haven't met him yet. His job required him to travel on a regular basis."

"He was found dead, too. Next to your sister."

The news was like a one-two punch. Not only had Stacey been murdered, but so had the new man in her life. His sister was a sweet woman, had been wonderful to Caden. Why would they be a target? It just didn't make any sense. Unless this Jonas guy was somehow responsible? Knowing his sister, he felt sure that must be the case. "Do you have any leads?"

"I can't discuss the investigation. I know this must be hard for you, losing your sister like this. I'm sorry for your loss." Was it his imagination or did her gaze soften? "The ME will do an autopsy in a few days, and you'll be notified when they're finished so you can make funeral arrangements. Did your sister live here?"

"Ah, yes, but not with me." It wasn't easy to concentrate while knowing his sister was gone forever. "There's a small living space off the back side of the lodge. But she often traveled to the other two properties, too."

"I see. Do you have a key to her living quarters?"

He nodded. "I haven't been in there without her permission. We mostly ate together in the dining room, or she came here to help with Caden." He rose and grabbed a key card from the counter, remembering how Stacey had trusted him.

She took it, then handed him a small, square business

card and rose to her feet. "Thanks. We'll check it out. Please call if you can think of anything else."

"I— Wait." He stood, too, once again moving Caden to his other arm. "This is a lot to process, but I want to see where she was found." He should put a small bouquet of flowers there in Stacey's memory.

Then realized he wasn't sure what his sister's favorite flowers were. She'd liked daisies as a girl, but now? No clue. He hadn't made time for many visits home during the past ten years he'd been in the army. Annette had preferred living in Seattle. He should have done better, and the guilt, on top of the load he already carried over Annette's death, nearly sent him to his knees.

He'd failed Stacey, just like he'd failed his wife.

"Not tonight, sorry. You can go after the crime scene has been fully processed. Come, Hutch." The officer and the large German shepherd headed for the door.

He followed, feeling sick at the realization his sister had been brutally murdered. First Annette's car crash and now Stacey. Waves of grief washed over him, but his army training helped him stay upright, to soldier forward. He walked Officer Hayes all the way to the elevator. "Please find the person who did this."

"We will." Her confidence was reassuring. "Again, I'm sorry for your loss. Take care of yourself, Luke. And Caden, too."

The elevator door opened, and she stepped inside. As the doors closed, he turned away, his thoughts mired in sorrow. And guilt. A flash of movement came at him from the left. He instinctively lifted his arm in self-defense, taking the brunt of the blow against his forearm, even as he curled his body around his son. Pain zinged through him, and he caught a glimpse of what looked like a baseball bat.

"Umph," he groaned, hitting the wall with a jarring thud. For a moment his vision blurred, then he caught sight of a dark figure disappearing down the stairs. That spurred him into action. He straightened. "Stop! Hey, stop!"

He wanted to give chase, but having Caden in his arms gave him pause. What if the assailant was armed with something else? A knife?

A gun?

His mind whirled. Was this assault related to his sister's murder?

And if so, why?

TWO

Hearing Luke's muffled grunt followed by a thud had Danica stabbing the elevator's door-open button. Thankfully the elevator hadn't started its descent, and the doors slid apart, revealing Luke standing with Caden.

"What happened?"

He waved a hand toward the stairs. "I was attacked..."

She didn't wait for him to finish. She quickly unleashed the dog. "Get him, Hutch!"

The shepherd sniffed the air, then took off. She ran to keep up with him. The stairs were narrow, and she peered over the railing hoping to catch a glimpse of the perp below.

At the second floor, Hutch paused to sniff at the narrow opening beneath the door then continued down to the first floor.

When they reached the landing, she cautiously opened the door, peering out for a moment before moving through. She passed four doorways leading to guest rooms, she assumed. A few steps later, they were in the rustic yet beautiful lobby.

A couple was sitting on a sofa in front of a massive stone fireplace, basking in the warmth of the fire as they looked at a map. No doubt planning their hiking path for the following day. There was another older couple coming inside through the wide lobby doors, their faces ruddy with the cold.

"Did anyone see a man or woman running past here?" Danica asked loudly.

Both the younger couple and the older shook their heads. "Like who?" the younger man asked.

"Anyone who seemed in a real hurry, possibly carrying something."

"No," the older woman said, moving closer to her husband.

Hutch sniffed around the lobby, then came back to sit beside her. "Come," she commanded, returning to the stairwell. The assailant must have disappeared through the second-floor doorway.

Upon opening that door, she found the hallway looked very similar to the one outside Luke Stark's door. There were four doors, two more than what had been on the third floor. Were these rooms as large as his? Based on the space between the doorways, she didn't think so. She made a mental note to ask Luke about that later. For now, she tried to imagine where the assailant had gone.

Into one of the rooms?

As she headed down the hallway, she noticed another stairwell on the opposite end. Without hesitation, she opened the door and headed down. Rather than going into the lobby, that doorway led directly outside.

For a long moment she stood on the threshold, peering into the dusky light. The Stark Lodge was in the middle of the wilderness, a solid two miles outside the town of Ashford and another three miles to Mount Rainier park.

In her gut, she suspected whoever had assaulted Luke was long gone. Unless the person was indeed staying there as a guest. Swallowing a sigh, she went back inside and took the stairs back up to the third floor.

She knocked on Luke's door. He immediately opened it, still holding Caden. She didn't know much about kids, although Luke's son was cute. Based on her own family situation, she never intended to go down that path, so she told herself to ignore Caden's handsome dad. And the adorable son.

"Doggy." Caden once again leaned toward the dog.

"How about you learn how to say Daddy?" Luke asked dryly.

She had to smile. "Are you okay? Did you get a good look at the assailant?"

"No, I didn't." Frustration underscored his tone. "I should have been paying closer attention, but I wasn't expecting someone to strike out at me with a baseball bat."

"Can you think of any reason for someone to do that?" she pressed. If the bat had hit Luke's head, he could have suffered a severe head injury. Maybe even death. It occurred to her that maybe the same person who'd killed his sister and Digby was now after Luke. Or maybe someone believed he was the one who murdered his sister and Digby and was seeking revenge. She stepped inside the suite, making sure Hutch had followed before closing the door behind her.

"You mean other than the fact that someone just murdered my sister and her boyfriend? No."

"Nothing like this happened before?"

"I'd tell you if it did." He glanced at his son, who was starting to fuss, his eyes looking sleepy. "Give me a minute to put Caden down in his crib."

"Okay." She bent to put Hutch back on leash, then walked over to the wide balcony doors to admire the view. It was too cold to sit out there now, but in summertime it would be incredible. The lodge was very nice. And could very well be the motive behind the murders.

She needed to verify Luke's alibi, but watching him with his son made it difficult to imagine him shooting his sister and Jonas Digby in cold blood.

Yet she didn't want to believe Mara had done that, either. And if not Luke or Mara, then who?

A text from Jasmin came in as she waited. It was a group text that included the team members who'd been in the park earlier and Donovan. She quickly scanned the new information.

Luke Stark will inherit Stacey's half of the three Stark properties, but they are heavily mortgaged, so not sure there's much to gain financially.

Interesting. Danica quickly texted back. Thanks for the information. What about her business partner, Eli Ballard? Any update?

The responding text came from Colt. Eli provided an alibi. I'm checking it out.

Okay, thanks. She turned her gaze back to the window, considering this new information.

Things were not looking good for Mara.

"Sorry about that." Luke's deep, husky voice broke into her thoughts. "He's out like a light."

"Great." She turned from the window to face him. "I need to know the name of every guest in the lodge."

Luke's eyebrows shot up. "You really think the assailant is a guest?"

"I don't know," she admitted. "But running their names would flag any with a criminal history."

"I'm the only long-term guest staying here. It wouldn't make sense for some weekend vacationer to strike out at me."

He had a point, although she preferred to cover all angles. Was it possible this was nothing more than a random event? Some bored but disturbed teenager with too much time on his or her hands? Looking at Luke, it was clear he wasn't seriously injured. But a baseball bat could be lethal, and the very real possibility of little Caden being hurt nagged at her.

Kids were supposed to be protected, not used as pawns in a dangerous game.

She warned herself not to go there. Her parents being violent toward each other wasn't pertinent to this case. Her personal life was better left in the past.

"I forgot to ask earlier. Do I, uh, need to identify Stacey's body?"

"Yes. I think we can do that tomorrow, though." She smiled kindly. "Maybe after I talk to Vera Johnson."

"Yeah, okay. Would you like a soft drink?" Luke gestured toward the small kitchenette. "I also have water."

"Oh, no, thank you." She flushed and rested her hand on Hutch's head. This was starting to feel too personal, and she couldn't have that. "We need to go. But I need those names from your desk clerk."

"Go where?" Luke's question surprised her. "You may as well stay here. I mean, at the lodge," he quickly clarified. "I can request a free room for you to use. We're not at capacity this early in spring." Even shadowed with grief, his green eyes were mesmerizing. "That way you'll be here when Vera comes in to work tomorrow morning."

"I—uh," she hesitated, realizing he was right. The cabin she lived in was provided by the park service and wasn't that far, but she was troubled by the attack. "I'll stay, but I'll pay my way. As a federal K-9 officer, I can't accept gratuities in the form of cash, food or lodging."

He held her gaze for a long moment. "I understand. I used to work for Uncle Sam, too." He glanced at the closed bedroom door, then went over to pick up a baby monitor receiver from a battery charger. "I'll walk you down to the lobby."

"That's okay, Hutch and I will be fine."

"Humor me." Luke tucked the baby monitor into his back pocket as he strode to the door. She kept Hutch close to her side as they took the elevator down.

"I still can't believe she's gone," Luke said in a low voice. "I should probably tell Jackie, the front desk clerk who works nights. Along with the rest of the staff. From what I saw, Stacey was well-liked. They'll be devastated by this news."

"How many staff?"

His brow puckered in a frown. "Seven. I already mentioned Vera, our cook, but there are also three servers for the restaurant, one housekeeper and two front desk clerks. Stacey used to help cover days off, and in summer she brought in college kids to help."

Made sense. "Hold off telling them about Stacey until tomorrow," she advised. "You said she travels? They won't miss her immediately. I'd like to talk to

Vera first, if that's okay. The news will likely spread quickly after that."

He nodded. The elevator dinged, and the doors opened. The young couple was gone now, as was the older couple. Luke walked with her to the front desk, where a young woman wearing the name tag Jackie sat reading a book.

"Jackie, this is a friend of mine, Danica Hayes. Could you please book her a room?"

"Sure thing." Jackie glanced curiously at Hutch, then tapped on the computer. "Two of our regular rooms are undergoing minor repairs. And Eve, our housekeeper, went home sick, so a couple of the rooms aren't ready. I only have a suite on the third floor, but you can have it for a regular room price."

Danica almost protested, but then realized this was likely standard procedure. Better to have rooms occupied than not.

"Thanks, that's fine." It was disconcerting to realize her room was next to Luke's. And that he'd referred to her as a friend.

She needed to call Donovan and Colt to update them on where she was with the case. Focusing on the murders would keep her from being distracted by the tall, dark, handsome Luke.

Jackie handed her a key, and Luke rode up the elevator with her. She'd need to take Hutch out one last time but decided to wait until she'd made her calls.

"Tell me about housekeeper Eve," she said. "Do you know much about her?"

"Eve Getty? She's old enough to be my mother," he responded. "Has arthritis in her hip, so she doesn't move too fast. Yet she's a hard worker, from what I can tell. Why?"

Likely not the assailant, or the killer, based on how quickly the person had escaped. "No reason."

He held her gaze for a long moment. "Good night, Danica."

She felt herself flush. "Ah, good night, Luke." She quickly unlocked the door and went inside.

The suite was just as nice as Luke's, including the same incredible view of Mount Rainier. She had an overnight bag and plenty of supplies for Hutch in her SUV just for this type of scenario.

She called Donovan to update him on Luke's alibi and her intent to stay the night, especially since she still needed to search Stacey's living quarters. Donovan agreed to update the rest of the team. As she headed to her SUV, her mind went back to the attack on Luke.

For some reason, she couldn't shake it off as a strange coincidence. The little boy's sweet face wouldn't leave her alone. She hated knowing he might have been hurt. Who would want to attack Luke? Stacey was murdered, but who sought to get Luke out of the picture, too? Stacey's business partner, Eli Ballard?

Jasmin said the properties were heavily mortgaged. The attack on Luke could be random, and not related to the murders, but she didn't believe in coincidence.

There had to be a link. And she was determined to find it.

Between his sister's murder and the attack in the hallway, Luke didn't sleep well. His heart ached for Stacey—she didn't deserve this. He wanted to go back, to have more time with her. To make up for his being gone so much over the past ten years. But it was too late now.

And the attack outside the elevator bothered him, too. Even though his role in the army had been that of a medic, he was also a soldier. It was humiliating to be caught off guard.

Never again, he thought grimly.

After losing Annette to a senseless car crash just three months ago, he'd become an instant single father. He knew about Caden, of course, but hadn't spent much time with him while being deployed overseas. He was granted an immediate honorable discharge from the army and had come to stay at the lodge, at Stacey's urging. Learning all there was to know about babies and getting to know his son had been the exact opposite from his life in the army.

Yet that wasn't a good excuse not to be on guard. Especially now that he knew about his sister's murder.

As morning dawned, he remembered Stacey saying something about Jonas Digby, the man in her life. She'd said that he made her want to be a better person.

A Christian, like Luke.

Or the way he used to be. Before the lies and cheating had soured him on love and marriage.

He'd just finished showering when he heard Caden babbling through the baby monitor—the greatest invention since sliced bread. After quickly tossing on some clothes, he went to get his son before his cheerful babbling turned into a full-fledged wail. One thing he'd quickly learned was his son liked to eat.

"Hey, big guy." He lifted Caden out of his crib. It was one the lodge had provided for him to use in the three-bedroom suite. "How about we get you changed and fed, hmm?"

His son mumbled something he couldn't decipher, then said, "Doggy."

"You'll see the doggy later," he said, hoping to make good on that promise. Just the thought of identifying his sister's body made him feel sick. He tried to push through his sorrow to focus on his son. "Can you say daddy? Dad-dy?"

"Doggy," Caden repeated, showing off his four new front teeth in a wide smile.

Most mornings he fed Caden here in the small kitchenette, but today he took the boy down to the dining room. He used the stroller because it would be easier once he and Danica headed to the ME's office. This would be the second time he'd have to perform the grim task. First Annette, now Stacey. No one should have to do such an awful thing twice in three months.

He pushed the grief aside. Caden deserved his full attention. The dining room wasn't large, roughly eight tables. There were only ten guest rooms—the two suites on the third floor, and four rooms each on the first and second floors.

The army had trained him to be an early riser, so he wasn't surprised to be the first guest up and about.

"Good morning."

He whirled at the sound of a female voice to find Danica standing there with Hutch. The pair had obviously just come in from outside. To his surprise, she was wearing jeans, a sweater and a quilted vest, her long blond hair loose around her face. She looked more woman than cop this morning, and he was annoyed at the flicker of attraction. He'd just lost his sister. Why was he allowing himself to be distracted?

He gave her a brief nod. "Hi. Join us for breakfast?"

"Sure. Is Vera here already?" She walked with him into the small dining room, looking around with curiosity.

"Yes, but she'll be in full cooking mode. You may want to wait for a bit." When Danica frowned, he added, "She's not going anywhere. We can eat first."

"Okay." With reluctance, she joined him. Hutch stretched out under the table, while he grabbed a high chair for Caden.

The early-morning server, Kim, came over to greet them. "Coffee?"

"Yes, please," he and Danica said at the same time.

He managed a smile as Kim filled the two mugs with coffee. He took a sip, noticing Danica drank hers black, too.

"Doggy, doggy," Caden said, banging on the table.

"It's the only word he knows," Luke said dryly. He opened a container of dry cereal and put some out for him.

"I'm sure that will change soon." She eyed him over the rim of her cup. "I'd like to show a picture of a woman to you and your staff, see if anyone recognizes her."

"They're not my staff," he protested. Although now that he thought about it, he supposed they were. Or half of them were. Did Eli and Stacey jointly manage the staff or did they have separate tasks? He didn't know the nuts and bolts of running the lodges, but understood he'd need to find out sooner than later. He knew Stacey and Eli often traveled between the three lodges. While his sister primarily stayed here in the living quarters not far from the kitchen, Eli lived at the lodge outside Olympia. They'd taken turns spending time at the third lodge near the North Cascades.

Clearly, he should have asked Stacey more questions about her role and Eli's, rather than being so focused on getting to know his son. Not that he'd ever imagined his sister would be murdered. He sighed and set down his mug. "Show me."

Danica swiped at her phone, then held it out for him. "Does she look familiar? Maybe you saw her hanging around?"

The woman on the screen had long dark hair and a pretty face, with bright green eyes. He shook his head. "No, sorry. But I haven't been out and about that much, either. Only when I take Caden for walks in his stroller. Being a full-time dad..." He hesitated, then thought better of complaining and simply added, "Has been keeping me busy. I had a lot to learn."

"I'm sure. Thanks anyway." Danica slipped her phone back in her pocket. "You don't mind if I ask the others, do you?"

"Of course not." He wanted to ask the woman's name but held his tongue. If she was a suspect, Danica wasn't going to give him any details.

"Where's Caden's mother?"

Danica's question hit him in the gut. "Ah, she passed away about twelve weeks ago. I— Uh, we married rather quickly when I was on leave between deployments, and she wasn't happy with the time I was forced to spend away from her." His gaze landed on his son, the best thing to have come out of his relationship with Annette. "Caden and I are still getting to know each other."

"I'm sorry, I didn't mean to pry." Her light brown eyes were full of compassion.

"You didn't. It's a logical question."

They ordered their food, which came fast, since they were the only ones in the dining room. Then Danica surprised him the second time that morning by folding her hands in her lap and bowing her head to pray.

Many of the guys who put their lives on the line during their tours overseas prayed. Luke used to do the same, but that practice changed when his hasty marriage had begun to split at the seams. He numbly realized he hadn't prayed once since returning Stateside.

"You're not a believer?" Danica asked.

"I was—still am, it's just…" He wasn't normally this awkward. "My relationship with God is shaky at the moment." A fact not helped by losing his sister. Why would God take both Annette and Stacey from him?

"I understand. Mine was, too. It's only been over the past few years that I've grown closer to Him." She smiled, then dug into her food.

Luke fed Caden some mashed banana mixed with his formula-made cereal. Then he gave the little boy a bottle. Caring for Caden helped keep him from dwelling on his loss.

"This is great," Danica said. "I can't wait to meet Vera. She has some awesome cooking skills."

"Here she comes now." Luke nodded to a sweet-faced woman who was pleasantly plump, wearing an apron and hair net covering her bright red curly hair.

"Luke, I can't believe you didn't bring your little angel to see me," she scolded. "Hi, Caden. How are you feeling today?"

"Bahahmbaa." Caden smiled his toothy grin. "Doggy."

"His teething seems better, thanks." Luke lightly rested a hand on Danica's arm. "This is K-9 officer Danica Hayes. She'd like to ask you a few questions."

"Me?" Vera looked shocked. "About what?"

"Do you remember what time Luke and Caden visited you in the kitchen yesterday?" Danica asked.

"Five o'clock. This little guy was having a rough time." Vera patted Caden's back. "I put a teething ring in the freezer, then listened as Luke read him a story about Clifford the Big Red Dog."

"Dog," Caden dutifully repeated. The book and now Hutch. No wonder the kid was focused on dogs.

"How long were the two of you together?" Danica asked.

"About an hour." Vera frowned. "What's this about?"

"I can't say just yet," Danica hastened to assure her. "I appreciate your time."

"Thanks, Vera. Breakfast was great," Luke added.

Vera looked suspicious but bent to press a kiss to Caden's head. "I'll talk to you later, Luke."

"She really likes you," Danica said.

"Nah, she really likes Caden." Then he frowned. "She wouldn't lie to give me an alibi."

"I'm sure she wouldn't." Danica wiped her mouth with a napkin. "How much do I owe you? I need to show this picture to your staff."

"They're not mine," he snapped. Then flushed. "Sorry, I'm still getting used to all this."

"I understand." Her eyes filled with compassion. "There's been a lot of change for you recently."

No kidding.

"More coffee?" At his nod, Kim filled their cups.

"Kim, can you tell me if you've seen this woman

around recently?" Danica held up her phone displaying the dark-haired woman's picture.

"I think so. Yes, I remember now. She was here just two days ago. Took a seat, but then changed her mind about eating."

Luke straightened in his seat. "Really?"

Danica frowned at him, then looked at Kim. "What time of the day?"

"I work the morning shift," Kim said. "I don't remember the exact time, maybe nine thirty?"

"Thank you." Danica lowered the phone. After Kim left, she turned to look at the front desk. "Who is that guy at the desk?"

"His name is Greg. He's the day-shift clerk. Again, I don't know much about the employees here." He gestured to her phone. "Is she a suspect?"

"Luke, I'm sorry, but I can't really talk about the case with you." Her gaze went back to Greg, and he knew she wanted to query him, too.

He set his napkin aside, plucked Caden from his seat and stood. "Come on, I'll introduce you."

Danica rose, and Hutch slithered out from beneath the table, unwilling to be left alone. He led the way across the lobby, lifting a hand to get Greg's attention.

"Greg, this is Officer Danica Hayes."

"Good morning. Have you seen this woman around recently?" She handed Greg the phone.

He nodded thoughtfully. "Sure did. She was here twice in the past week."

Twice? Luke's heart thudded in his chest. He assumed the woman was a suspect. His sister's potential murderer was here twice in the past week?

Danica's expression indicated she was surprised at the news, too. "When exactly did you see her?"

"Two days ago, she was here in the morning, but earlier in the week she was here midafternoon." Greg shrugged. "I didn't pay attention to the times. I only remember her because she's so pretty."

"Thank you." Danica turned away, and he could see the wheels turning in her mind.

No doubt the woman was a suspect in his sister's murder. But why? What did it all mean?

And the most important question of all—was Caden safe?

THREE

Dread seeped through her belly. Mara Gilmore had been at the Stark Lodge twice in the past week. Why? To spy on her ex-boyfriend's new girlfriend? Had she been here the day Stacey and Jonas headed out to the park? She could have easily followed the pair, then shot them.

The evidence against their crime scene tech was difficult to ignore. Granted, most of it was circumstantial at this point. Maybe the autopsy would reveal DNA or other proof that would clear Mara.

After questioning the lodge's staff individually, she informed them about Stacey's death. She watched each person's reaction carefully, doing her best to look for signs of guilt or relief, but all she saw in their features was shock and sorrow at the news.

The search she'd done of Stacey's private rooms earlier that morning along with the Park Ranger techs, didn't reveal much. She was surprised there wasn't even a picture of Stacey and Jonas Digby together. The park crime scene techs had swept for prints, but she didn't hold out much hope they'd find anything significant.

They didn't have any substantial clues to work with.

Danica sent up a silent prayer for God to show them the way to uncovering the truth. Letting go of her concern over Mara's involvement, she focused on the present. Now that she'd validated Luke's alibi, she needed to take him to identify his sister's body. Once those tasks were finished, she could get back to the crime scene.

"I don't understand what's happening," Luke said as they returned to the dining room. He set Caden in his stroller, then turned to face her. "You need to straight up tell me if my son is in danger."

She hesitated. Normally she wouldn't reveal any details of the case to a civilian, but looking at the little boy, she knew she had to give Luke something. Plus, he was a victim's next of kin. "This woman in the photograph is a former girlfriend of Jonas Digby. If this is a crime of passion or revenge, you and Caden should be safe. But I'll be honest—it's too early in the investigation to say for sure. Especially given the attack against you last night. I don't know how that figures in with the murders."

He held her gaze for a long moment before nodding. "Thanks. That helps."

She secretly wished she could help more, but she'd already told him more than she should. After paying for their respective meals, they headed into the lobby. Hutch glanced often at Caden riding in the stroller beside him, as if understanding his role was partially to protect him.

"The morgue is in Olympia. It's a ninety-minute drive." She glanced at Caden. "Do you need to bring extra supplies along for your son?"

"Good idea. Wait here, I'll be back soon." Luke pushed the stroller toward the elevator. She gazed around the lobby of the lodge, impressed with the combination of cozy warmth and luxury.

The rooms were pricey, but she was glad to have experienced the place for herself. In her opinion, there were only two viable theories of the crime: Mara had killed Jonas and Stacey out of anger and revenge, or someone else had done the deed, which was likely related to the three properties Stacey co-owned with Eli Ballard.

She tried to come up with a third possibility, but considering the victims didn't have criminal backgrounds, she couldn't think of one. And how did Luke's attack fit in? The attack coming so close to Stacey and Jonas's murders, she felt certain they were connected.

Donovan had told them to keep an open mind. Since she'd be in Olympia, she made a mental note to stop in at headquarters to update him on how two lodge staff members had recognized Mara. Later that day, she'd return to question the late shifters.

"We're ready." Luke returned pushing the stroller. He'd bundled Caden in a blue snowsuit and hat. "Should we drive separately?"

"No need. I have to return to the lodge anyway." She turned to walk outside. "We'll take my SUV—it's set up for Hutch."

"Okay." Luke pushed Caden's stroller outside.

She hesitated, remembering the strange assault on Luke and the stairway that led outside. "Give me a minute to walk around the property first."

"Why?" Luke asked with a frown.

"Just checking it out. I looked around last night but want to see it again in the daylight."

Luke shrugged and took a step back, giving her room to move past him.

There was a shoveled walkway leading all the way around the sprawling three-story lodge. With Hutch at her side, she searched for new footprints in the snow but didn't find any. There was a side door on either side of the building, along with a door in the back near the kitchen. There was also a small room jutting out where Stacey lived. The area around that wasn't disturbed. Whoever had come out through the side door last evening must have stayed on the path.

It was strange, though, since the lodge was rather isolated out here. It was located at the halfway point between Ashford and the Nisqually entrance to Mount Rainier park. The assailant had to either have a room here or live in Ashford. The town of Ashford was very small, fewer than five hundred residents, and the town primarily existed for tourists visiting the area.

She quickly returned to where Luke stood near Caden's stroller. Hutch sniffed at Caden, then sat looking at him curiously, making the baby laugh.

She smiled, thinking Hutch and Caden looked cute together.

"Maybe I should get a dog," Luke drawled. "Caden clearly adores Hutch."

"You absolutely should, but a puppy and a baby would dramatically increase your workload," she warned. "You may want to consider getting an older dog from a shelter rather than a puppy that has to be trained." She gestured toward the small parking lot. "My SUV is that black one over there."

"I see it." Luke pushed the stroller forward.

She opened the back for Hutch as Luke took the

stroller apart. Amazingly, the stroller came apart in two pieces, the seat portion functioning as a car seat for the baby. Luke took a moment to secure the car seat, then strapped Caden in. Hutch pressed his nose against the back crate area near the baby.

Danica slid behind the wheel, glancing at Luke. "Ready?"

"Yeah." He smiled wryly. "Sorry, it's always a production traveling with a baby."

"Not that much different than traveling with a dog." She pulled out onto the highway. "I don't want to badger you about your sister, Luke. I'm sure this has been a shock, but anything you can remember about her recent activities would be helpful."

He was quiet for a long moment. "I told you she mentioned Jonas Digby as her new boyfriend. She wanted me to meet him, because he was a Christian and Jonas was important to her. I feel terrible I can't tell you anything more. We spent some time together getting caught up, but she was busy running the lodges and with her new boyfriend, while I was focused on Caden."

"I get that. But if anything else comes to you, please don't hesitate to let me know."

"I won't. I want the person responsible to rot in jail for the rest of his or her life." Luke raked a hand through his chocolate-brown hair. "Sorry, that sounded harsh. But Stacey was a good person. She didn't deserve this."

"I know she didn't."

They drove in silence for a while.

"I remember something else." Luke abruptly broke the silence. "About two weeks ago, Stacey and I had lunch together. That's when she told me about Jonas, but

I think she also said something about how I'd be proud of how hard she's working to deal with some problems."

Her pulse kicked up a notch. "What kind of problems?"

Luke flushed and shook his head. "I didn't ask. To be honest, Stacey tended to do things the easy way, so I assumed it was something she'd ignored until recently. Then Caden threw up, ending our conversation." There was an edge of frustration underlying his tone. "I wish I'd paid more attention to my sister. I should have talked to her more than I did. You always think you have time, you know? Then you don't. I can't help but wonder if the problems she'd mentioned are related to her murder?"

"It's possible, but don't be too hard on yourself. It's easy to second-guess your actions after the fact. There's no way you could have known Stacey was in danger."

"But I didn't ask her about anything. Not about her new boyfriend, not what problems she was dealing with or what responsibilities she had related to running the three properties." She could tell he was torturing himself over the sudden loss of his sister.

"Monday-morning quarterback," she reminded him. "Besides, look at it this way. If Stacey thought she was in danger, she would have told you, right?"

Another long minute passed. "In danger? Yeah, I think so. She knew I was dealing with a lot between losing Annette and becoming a full-time father to Caden, but she also knew I spent several tours overseas as a soldier and medic. I believe she'd have mentioned feeling unsafe."

"I think so, too." She concentrated on the road, as she considered what sort of problem Stacey had mentioned.

General problems like being short-staffed in running the lodges or running at less than full occupancy?

Or something more?

Had Jonas told Stacey about his former girlfriend, Mara? Had the two women met? Willow was close with Mara, and she thought about meeting up with her later to find out more about the relationship between the former couple.

They had to stop once at a rest area so Luke could change Caden's diaper. She let Hutch out to take care of business, too. When they returned to the SUV, Luke set the diaper bag on the floor of the back seat. "I think I finally mastered this diaper bit. For the first week, I put them on backward."

She burst out laughing, then clapped a hand over her mouth. "I'm sorry, that wasn't funny."

"Oh, it's funny *now*," he said dryly. "But not so much when I had a giant mess to take care of every day."

"If it makes you feel any better, I probably wouldn't have any clue which way to put a diaper on, either."

That made him smile.

Her teammate Colt Maxwell called. She glanced at Luke, debating if she should answer. "Hey, Colt, I'm in the car with the victim's brother. We're heading to Olympia to identify Stacey's body."

"Okay, give me a call when you're finished. I have an update."

"Will do." She disconnected from the call.

"An update on my sister's murder?" Luke asked.

"I don't know." She squirmed a bit in her seat. "I'm sorry, Luke, but I can't discuss details of the case with you."

"Yeah, yeah. I'm just the victim's brother." There

was a hint of annoyance in his tone. She did her best to ignore it.

If the situation were reversed, she'd feel the same way.

They made it to Olympia without a problem, although she could feel Luke grow tense as they approached the city.

She navigated the streets until they came to the city morgue. After parking, she turned to face Luke. "Are you ready?"

"Not really. I hate having to take Caden inside, but I can't leave him out here, either. Let's go." He didn't hesitate, and she could easily imagine he'd approached his overseas missions the same way.

He carried Caden rather than reassembling the stroller/car seat combo. The medical examiner's staff were still preparing Stacey's body. There was a window covered by a shade. While they waited, she stepped back to call Colt quickly. "What's up?"

"Eli Ballard has an airtight alibi for the time frame of the murders," Colt informed her.

She blew out a breath. "You're sure?"

"Yeah. I wish I wasn't. Everyone around Eli claims he's a great guy, super nice and helpful. The guy who gave him the alibi doesn't have a criminal history, either. I gotta say, things are looking bad for Mara."

"I know. Thanks, Colt. We'll talk more later."

She quickly disconnected, just as the staff inside the morgue lifted the shade.

Luke stepped up to the window, his expression seemingly carved in stone. He cradled Caden on his shoulder so the baby was looking at her and Hutch rather than through the window. Thankfully, the baby adored the dog and stayed focused on Hutch. The staff member lifted the sheet, exposing Stacey's face.

"Yes. That's my sister, Stacey Ann Stark." His voice hitched a bit on her middle name.

"Thank you, Luke." She nodded at the staff member, who replaced the sheet, then closed the blind.

He didn't say anything else until they were outside. Then he turned to face her, his eyes swimming with grief. "Promise me you'll find out who did this."

"I promise you that our entire team will do our best to find out who did this."

He closed his eyes for a minute, then turned away to place Caden back in the car seat. She knew it wasn't what he'd wanted to hear.

But she wasn't about to make a promise she couldn't keep.

It wasn't the first dead body he'd seen—as an army medic he'd witnessed far too many. Fellow soldiers who died of terrible injuries in battle.

But seeing his sister had been worse. Stacey hadn't signed up to be a soldier, to put her life on the line. She was younger than him by four years and had had her whole life ahead of her.

Now she was gone.

Glancing at Danica, he squelched a flash of anger. He'd noticed she'd made a phone call while they were waiting in the morgue and knew she had new information about the murder. He didn't care about the rules—he wanted to know everything she did.

He slammed the car door with more force than needed. Then felt guilty for letting his anger get the better of him.

"I need to make another quick stop, if you don't mind," she said.

"That's fine." He was hardly in a position to argue, and thankfully, Caden seemed to enjoy car rides. He glanced over his shoulder to see Caden turning his head to see Hutch in the wire crate in the cargo area. Hutch tilted his head at the baby, making his son giggle.

His anger faded in the face of his son's smile. He had to trust the K-9 officers would find the person, likely the dark-haired woman, responsible for killing Stacey.

In the meantime, he'd have to plan her funeral. And figure out what, if anything, he should do related to running the lodges. Helping in that respect was the least he could do for Stacey. Maybe he could keep an eye on the one he was currently staying in near Mount Rainier, while Stacey's business partner looked after the other two.

"What about Eli Ballard?" He shifted in his seat to look at Danica. "Do I have to worry about him being involved?"

"His alibi checks out, so I don't think so." She kept her gaze on the road.

He narrowed his gaze, trying to read between the lines. "I don't want my son in danger."

"I don't want that, either." Now she glanced at him. "I would never put a child in harm's way."

"Okay, then." He had to let it go, although trusting her wasn't easy.

Annette had lied to him, more than once. About loving him, about who she was seeing while he was overseas. He would have asked for a DNA test to prove Caden was his son if it wasn't for the identical half-moon shaped birthmark Caden had on his back, the same one he had. Not to mention, Caden looked just like him when he was young.

A few minutes later, Danica pulled over. "This is our K-9 unit headquarters." Danica gestured to a majestic two-story stone building located on Twelfth Avenue. The place looked nicer than any other police headquarters he'd ever seen. Certainly better than what the army had to offer. "Do you mind waiting out here? It won't take me long. I'll take Hutch with me."

"Sure." She released Hutch from the back. They headed up the stairs and disappeared inside the building. He pushed out of the car, then unbuckled Caden from the back. He needed to stretch his legs and figured his son could use a change of scenery. He didn't bother with the stroller, though, simply carrying his son up and down the sidewalk, pointing out things for him to say. "Car. Can you say car? How about truck? Look, there's a bike. Can you say bike?"

"Doggy," Caden shouted.

"Yeah, I'm aware you've got that one down pat." He tried a few more things, then gave up. *That's it, no more Clifford the Big Red Dog books.* Maybe he'd find Caden a book about a boy and his daddy. That might work.

He was heading back to the SUV when he heard Danica talking to another woman with long brown hair who also had a dog with her. The K-9 was smaller than Hutch and looked like a pointer with brown and white coloring. "I don't know why Mara was at the Stark Lodge. That's why I'm asking you, Willow."

Luke froze.

"Maybe she just wanted to talk to Stacey," Willow responded. She was dressed in the same green K-9 uniform that Danica had worn the day before. "Or maybe she was trying to find Jonas to talk to him about what went wrong in their relationship. There are any number of innocent reasons for her to have been there. It doesn't mean she killed anyone."

"Chief says we're to keep an open mind, and I am," Danica said in a reassuring tone. "But that also means uncovering the truth, no matter how painful that might be."

"I hear you." Willow sounded glum. "Star and I need to head back. I'll talk to you later."

The two separated, and Luke stepped forward to approach Danica. She grimaced when she saw him.

"I'm sorry," he quickly apologized. "By the time I realized what was happening, it was too late."

"I'm sure." Danica's voice was dry. "Let's hit the road."

The drive back seemed to take much longer. Maybe because the easy camaraderie between them was gone. He hadn't intended to eavesdrop.

Yet he wasn't sorry to have learned the dark-haired woman's name was Mara. Or that Mara was Jonas Digby's ex.

When they arrived at the lodge, Danica shifted into Park then turned to face him. "You can head inside. I have some things to do."

"Yeah, okay. Thanks." It took him a few minutes to get Caden out of the seat. He had to set his son on the floor of the car next to the diaper bag to put the car seat and stroller contraption back together.

Clever design, if a bit of a pain. He set Caden in the stroller moving it up along the sidewalk, so that he could close the car door. The wind carried it another foot or so and Caden laughed as if enjoying the ride.

It made him smile to hear the boy laugh. A good reminder that as much as he missed Stacey, he needed to continue building his relationship with his son. Which meant leaving the investigating of his sister's murder to the police.

Up ahead, he noticed an older couple struggling to open the front door of the lodge. The wind was pushing it shut. With Danica still in the SUV, he figured it would be fine to leave Caden in his stroller for a moment. He hurried over to help them.

"Oh, thank you so much," the woman gushed.

"You're welcome." He waited for her partner to walk inside, too, then glanced back to where he'd left Caden in the stroller.

The stroller—and Caden—were gone.

"Caden? Caden!" His heart thudded painfully against his ribs as he ran back to the sidewalk, glancing frantically back and forth. He'd only been gone a minute or two. *"Caden!"*

"What's wrong?" Danica jumped from the SUV.

"Caden, the stroller…" Then he glimpsed a woman wearing a black puffy coat and a black knit cap pushing Caden's stroller away from the lodge. "Hey, you! Stop! That's my son!"

At his shout, the woman shoved the stroller, sending it careening toward a snowbank.

Then she ran.

FOUR

Spinning around, Danica hit her key fob to automatically open the back hatch to release Hutch. The K-9 shepherd jumped down, and she pointed down the sidewalk. "Get her!"

Hutch bounded after the woman in the long black puffy coat. Danica ran as fast as she could behind him. Luke was sprinting down the sidewalk toward the stroller.

Lord, keep Caden safe in Your care!

Unfortunately, the mystery woman had a head start. She reached an open door of a black sedan car and slid behind the wheel. She managed to slam the door in time to prevent Hutch from getting to her.

"Stop! Police!" Danica shouted.

The woman revved the engine and took off, the back end of the sedan swerving a bit as she fought to gain control. Danica peered at the license plate only to find it was covered in mud. That had to have been done on purpose.

"Come, Hutch."

Her partner wheeled toward her and loped back to

her side. She glanced over to where Luke was bent over Caden. "Is he okay?"

"I think so." His words were muffled, and she realized he had the baby cradled in his arms, his face buried against the little boy's head.

"I'm going after her. Come, Hutch." Danica jogged toward the SUV. The rear hatch was still open, and her partner quickly hopped inside. After closing the door, she hurried around to slide behind the wheel. Seconds later, she peeled out of the parking lot.

There wasn't a lot of traffic here this time of the year, however, the curvy, often ice-covered roads made it impossible to go too fast. Using her hands-free function, she called the local police to put out an alert for a black sedan with muddy license plates. "The driver tried to kidnap a baby in a stroller."

"Kidnap? That's terrible. Do you have a make or model?" the dispatcher asked.

She thought for a moment, visualizing the sedan in her mind. "I believe it's a Honda—I saw the *H* emblem on the back of the vehicle. Four doors, but I can't say which model."

"That helps. We'll get the BOLO out," the dispatcher assured her.

"Thanks." She continued driving. There were only two side roads the woman could have used to escape. Determined, she checked them both, going in all directions.

After nearly ten minutes of driving, she had to admit defeat. She'd lost the perp.

Mentally kicking herself for not reacting quicker, she found a spot to make a U-turn and headed back to the lodge. Between the attack the night before, and this kidnapping attempt, it was clear Luke and Caden were in danger.

Yet she didn't understand the motive behind both attempts. And how did this relate to Stacey Stark's murder?

At this point, she didn't see the connection, but the timing alone suggested there was one. She just needed to find it.

One thing was clear—she couldn't walk away. The woman in the long black puffy coat had clearly intended to take Caden from his father. What if she or someone else close to her tried again?

Time to call her boss. "Donovan? It's Danica. I just witnessed a kidnapping attempt. A woman with a long black puffy coat and a dark hat grabbed the stroller with Caden Stark inside." She explained the particulars, then added, "She was heading toward a car, but when Luke shouted at her, she pushed the stroller toward the snowbank and jumped into a black Honda sedan. I sent Hutch after her, but she got away. I tried to trail her in my vehicle, too, and alerted the locals, but I'm concerned about the boy's safety."

"You think this is related to Stacey Stark's murder?"

"I believe so. I'm not sure how or why, but the coincidence is too much to ignore."

"I agree. Could the woman have been Mara?"

Danica thought about that. "I didn't see the perp's face or hair, but the build seemed different. I don't think it was Mara, but I can't say with absolute certainty she wasn't."

"Okay. I'll send Colt and Sampson over—they're out at the Mount Rainier crime scene. Maybe you can pick up the perp's scent."

"Thanks." Sampson was a cadaver dog, so he had a good nose for scents. Usually for dead people, but she'd take all the backup she could get. "I would like to stay at the lodge for a few days, until we understand what's going on."

"Good plan," Chief Fanelli agreed. "Let me know if either of the K-9s come up with anything."

"Will do." She disconnected from the call and pulled back into the parking lot. There was no sign of Luke, Caden or the stroller. She'd been gone long enough that they'd probably gone back to the suite.

Sliding out from behind the wheel, she ran around to release Hutch, then headed inside. Rather than stopping at the front desk, she took the stairwell up the three flights to Luke's room.

"Luke?" She rapped on the door. "Are you in there?"

Seconds ticked by before the door opened. Luke still had Caden in his arms, as if unwilling to let his son go. His grim expression made her heart ache. He stepped back so she and Hutch could come inside. "Did you find her?"

"I'm afraid not." She closed the door behind her. "Caden's not hurt?"

"He seems okay." Luke blew out a breath, then crossed over to sit on the sofa. "It's my fault. I'm a terrible dad. I left the stroller on the sidewalk to help the older couple with the door. I let him get kidnapped."

"It's not your fault. You probably assumed it was fine since I was right there in my vehicle—you had no way of knowing I was looking down to read texts from my team about the case." She shook her head. "You'd think a baby in a stroller would be safe here, especially in broad daylight." She gave Hutch the hand signal to sit, then went over to join him at the sofa. "I'm the one who should have been more alert. If I had noticed earlier, I'm sure Hutch would have gotten her." She managed a wry smile. "Normally he gets his man, or in this case, his woman."

Luke didn't smile in return. "I almost lost him," he whispered.

"I know." She could only imagine what those few minutes of fearing the worst had felt like. "But the good news is that he's fine. The local cops have issued a BOLO—be on the lookout—for a black Honda sedan."

The news seemed to ease some of his concern. "Maybe I should leave. Head back to Seattle."

Oddly, her heart squeezed painfully in her chest. "Is that where you normally live?"

"Yeah, briefly." He sighed. "Being in the army meant traveling a lot. I met my wife in Seattle, and we got married too quickly. I don't think of the city as home, but why stay here if Caden is in danger?"

Understanding where he was coming from, she placed a reassuring hand on his arm. "Luke, I already spoke to my boss. I'm going to stay here to protect you and Caden. I honestly think the best way to keep you both safe is to figure out who is behind this. My boss is sending my teammate Colt and his K-9, Sampson, here, too. We're going to check things out."

"You really think you can find the woman responsible?" Luke raised his tortured gaze to hers.

"We can try. Leaving isn't the answer. What if the woman in the long black puffy coat somehow follows you and Caden to Seattle?"

"I don't see how she could do that."

"We don't know who she is," she reminded him.

"Are you sure you don't know anyone who would want to take him?"

He shook his head. "No. My parents are dead, and same goes for my wife's. Annette never knew her dad—apparently he didn't stick around—but her mother died several years ago."

"Aunts? Great-grandparents?" She pushed the issue because, in her experience, most kidnapping cases were perpetrated by family members. Normally a custody battle between spouses, but maybe someone from Luke or Annette's past felt they'd be a better parent to Caden.

"I think Annette had an aunt who lives in California, but I've never met her. She and Annette weren't close." He shook his head. "I wish I could be more helpful. I want that woman found more than anyone."

"I know." For a moment she considered Mara as the suspect. The woman who'd run off was definitely larger than the crime scene tech and had worn a different colored winter coat. Mara could have used a disguise, but why would she want to kidnap Stacey Stark's brother's baby? Everything came back to motive. Mara had motive to kill Stacey and Jonas, but getting dumped and trying to kidnap Stacey's baby nephew didn't seem related. Anything was possible, though.

Still, this gave her hope Mara was innocent and there was something going on here.

Her phone vibrated, and she recognized Colt's name on the screen. He'd sent a text saying he was down in the lobby. She gently squeezed Luke's arm, then rose to her feet. "I need to head back outside to meet with Colt and Sampson."

"Good. I hope you find something."

She started for the door, then stopped as her gaze fell

on the stroller. The woman had no doubt worn gloves, but her scent could still be on the stroller's handle. It wasn't the optimal scent source, yet it was better than nothing. "I'm going to take the stroller, okay?"

"Why?" He appeared interested in her thought process.

"It's possible the kidnapper's scent may be on the stroller handle." She hesitated, not wanting to give him a false sense of security. "She only held it briefly, likely while wearing gloves, and we typically use clothing for a scent source, so don't get your hopes up. This may not work."

"I understand." He stood and walked toward her. Caden wiggled in his arms. "Go ahead. It's worth a try."

"It is." She turned to her K-9 partner. "Come, Hutch."

The shepherd came to stand beside her. She gestured to the handle of the stroller and thought of a name for the scent that wouldn't frighten the guests in the lodge. "This is Blue. Seek! Seek Blue!"

Hutch followed her hand with his snout, sniffing along the stroller's handle. She trusted her K-9's keen nose, but would he be able to narrow in on the correct scent? She hoped and prayed he could.

"Luke, will you get the door for me?"

He hurried over. Touching only the sides of the stroller, she pushed it out the door and into the elevator. Luke watched her and Hutch for a long moment as the elevator doors slid closed.

In the lobby, she quickly joined Caden and Sampson. "The only scent source is the handle of the stroller," she informed them. "I'd like to use Hutch to check the interior of the lodge. Would you and Sampson mind checking outside?"

"Will do." Colt gave his bloodhound a few moments to pick up the scent from the handle.

Danica didn't wait. "Seek! Seek Blue!"

The K-9 went to work, first sniffing the air, then lowering his nose to the ground. Danica stayed back near the main entrance, giving him room. If this didn't work, she'd have to hope the BOLO would find the black sedan.

Unfortunately, two flimsy leads weren't much to work with.

Caden was happy to play with his toys, which helped ease Luke's mind over the kidnapping attempt. Thankfully, Caden hadn't understood the danger he'd been in.

But Luke did. And no matter what Danica tried to tell him, he knew his lack of attention had almost cost him his son.

He hung his head for a moment, battling guilt, then stood abruptly. Sitting here, ruminating over the kidnapping, and grieving the loss of his sister, wasn't helpful. Ten years in the army meant he was used to being active. Doing something important.

He paced the length of the suite, wondering what, if anything, Danica and her K-9 would find. He thought back to the attack outside the elevator. Being hit by the baseball bat had sent him reeling into the wall, but now that he considered it more closely, he felt the force behind the blow hadn't been as lethal as he'd expected. It probably hadn't been wielded by a man, as he'd first assumed.

But a woman. Likely the same woman who'd rolled Caden down the sidewalk toward her car.

"Doggy!" Caden had the Clifford book in his hands. "Doggy!"

"That's right." The walls seemed to be closing in on him. As much as he wanted Caden to be safe, he couldn't just sit there doing nothing.

Besides, if he and Caden weren't safe with two cops and their K-9s nearby, then they weren't safe anywhere.

"Come on, slugger." He scooped the little boy into his arms, taking a minute to nuzzle his neck. The scent of baby shampoo made him smile. "Let's go find that doggy."

"Bahwaha," Caden babbled.

"You got that right," Luke agreed, wishing for the umpteenth time he had a clue what Caden was trying to say.

His senses were on high alert, as if he were moving through the desert overseas rather than what should have been a safe lodge. His soldier instincts had him using the empty elevator rather than the stairwell. If the baseball bat attacker trapped them in the stairwell, there wouldn't be enough room to maneuver and escape. Not without risking an injury to Caden.

Putting his son in even the slightest danger wasn't an option.

The doors opened on the lobby level. He swept a gaze over the immediate area. A few guests lingered nearby, but he recognized them from the previous day.

Seeing them, though, reminded him that he hadn't gotten Danica the list of all guest names. He found himself staring at the female guests. He hadn't seen the kidnapper's face, so he couldn't guess her age, but she'd had a stocky build, which could be partially due to the puffy coat.

A few of the guests smiled at him. He'd discovered Caden attracted a lot of attention—strangers cooed at him often when they saw him, declaring him to be so cute.

Which he was, but after the kidnapping attempt, these people smiling at Caden made him scowl.

He caught sight of Danica and Hutch near the front doors of the lobby. He didn't want to interfere with Danica's search but was curious about how well this would work. His experience with K-9 dogs was limited to the bomb-sniffing dogs he'd encountered while overseas. They had only been trained for gunpowder and explosives, not to find people the way Hutch was trying to do. The idea of getting one specific scent from the stroller handle seemed far-fetched, but he was no expert. Caden's stroller was sitting off to the side, ready, he guessed, to be used again for a scent source if needed.

"Seek Blue," he heard Danica say. He'd been curious about her use of the word *Blue* but had held his tongue.

He approached from the side, keeping well out of Hutch's way. Danica frowned when she saw him.

"I won't get in the way," he promised in a low voice. "But I couldn't sit doing nothing."

"I understand." A fleeting smile teased her features, but then her attention went back to the K-9.

The dog sniffed all the way around the front doors of the lobby. Luke wondered where her backup was. She'd mentioned a cop named Colt and his K-9, Sampson. Turning a bit toward the window, he scanned the area outside. It didn't take long to catch a glimpse of a tall, blond man wearing the dark green K-9 uniform, walking behind a bloodhound.

Hutch abruptly spun away from the wall and trotted

across the lobby. Luke felt his pulse kick up with anticipation. The expression on Danica's face was bland, revealing no hint of her thoughts.

"Dogs can pick up on our emotions," she warned in a calm tone. "Your scent is likely on the stroller, too. I'm hoping he's picking up the most recent scent different from yours, which he'd recognize from the suite. Stay back, so he doesn't get confused."

"Okay." He shifted Caden to his other arm and remained where he was.

"Doggy," Caden said with glee. He leaned toward Hutch, but Luke tightened his grip. Maybe coming down wasn't a good idea—he didn't want his son to disturb the dog. Yet Hutch didn't look at Caden; he was focused on the task at hand.

Hutch and Danica made a great team.

Danica slowly strolled behind Hutch as he sniffed along the front lobby desk, then veered toward the seating area off to the right of the registration counter.

The dog garnered attention, but the guests didn't reach out to touch him. Probably because the large brown-and-tan German shepherd was not only at work but intimidating.

He'd be worried if Hutch was chasing after him, he thought with a wry grin.

The dog went over toward the large fireplace, continuing his exploration of the lobby. He didn't stop for long, though. Soon, he went into the dining room. At first he sniffed around the doorway, then continued inside.

Was Danica right about one of the guests being involved? The canine moved faster now, weaving between the tables. Had the scent of food enticed him in that direction? A couple of the guests looked surprised as Hutch swiftly moved past them.

Danica picked up her pace, too, which was enough to have him trailing behind her.

Hovering in the opening, he noticed Hutch spent a lot of time near the doorway to the kitchen. Then the large dog sat and turned to look at Danica with an intense gaze.

"Good boy, Hutch." She lavished praise on the dog, then pressed the door open to peek inside. She quickly closed the door, then tossed a stuffed animal in the air. The long, floppy ears made him think of a rabbit.

Hutch caught it midair, then shook the toy with his mouth playfully. She quickly led him out of the dining area and into the lobby, where he had more room to play.

"Good boy, Hutch," she said again, smiling as he ran around with the rabbit clenched between his teeth.

"He found something?" Luke went over to stand near Danica.

Danica looked thoughtful. "I think he found Blue."

"Why Blue?" he asked, perplexed.

She flushed. "We try not to give unknown subjects a person type of name—it's too confusing, especially if we discover the perp's real name. We use colors or things. People tend not to overreact when they hear a dog is searching for Blue."

He glanced back to the dining room, where the few guests had resumed eating. "He found the kidnapper's scent in there?"

"Hutch has been doing this for the past five years, four of them with this unit." She met his gaze head-on. "It's possible he found your kidnapper's scent near the kitchen door. I can't take him into the kitchen, though, because there was a strong scent of bleach, which can ruin Hutch's ability to track. Regardless, the scent could belong to a guest who went to lodge a complaint about the food, but we also need to rule out any of the lodge staff members being involved."

A staff member. It seemed inconceivable that one of the employees here would try to kidnap his son. Hutch sat between him and Danica and when Caden tried to pet the dog, he warned his son. "No, Caden."

He was once again torn between staying or heading to Seattle.

Yet watching Hutch tip his head side to side, making the little boy giggle, Luke knew the safest place for his son was here.

Under Danica and Hutch's protection.

FIVE

Colt pushed through the main entrance to the lodge with his K-9, Sampson, trotting at his side. Seeing Luke and Caden, he smiled, then said, "I'm sorry to say we came up with nothing outside. How about you? Did Hutch find anything?"

"Yes, Hutch alerted near the door going into the kitchen," Danica admitted. "But that doesn't help narrow things down. Could be a current or previous guest, or one of the staff. Frankly, since he didn't alert at other places in the dining room, I'm leaning toward a previous guest. Everyone, even the cook has been out here. The servers put on a lot of miles throughout the dining room each day, so Hutch would have alerted in multiple places if the perp was one of them."

"A previous server, maybe?" Colt asked.

She glanced questioningly at Luke, who nodded slowly. "There was some staff turnover earlier this year, but they lost a server just two weeks ago, a woman named Rhonda Fern. Stacey made it sound like she had to let Rhonda go. She didn't replace her because she only brings—er, brought in additional help during the peak seasons."

"We'll look into this Rhonda Fern." It felt good to have a possible lead. "And I'll need that list of current and previous guest names, too."

"I know, I'll get those to you ASAP," Luke agreed.

"No time like the present." Glancing toward the front desk, she noticed Greg, the clerk from yesterday, was on duty again today.

"Need anything else from Sampson?" Colt asked.

"I don't think so. I'm planning to stay here at the lodge for the next couple of days, until we figure out who is responsible for this kidnapping attempt."

"You're getting a vacation while the rest of us work, huh?" Colt teased. When she rolled her eyes, he added, "I'm heading back to the crime scene to see if Sampson can pick up anything else. There's a storm rolling in later this evening, so we don't have a lot of time. They're predicting four to six inches of snow overnight."

Snow in April was a normal occurrence at Mount Rainier, so she wasn't surprised by the change in weather. "Sounds good. Thanks for the heads-up."

Colt nodded at Luke, flashed a wide smile at Caden, then said, "Give a shout if you need anything."

"I will, thanks." She was grateful to have the support of her team.

"You and Colt seem to work well together." Luke eyed her curiously. "Have you known him long?"

She tilted her head. "Four years, and yes, we get along well. Colt is like the older brother I never had." The statement was true, but the mere mention of her troubled childhood instantly sent her to a dark place.

A terrible situation that no child should be forced to endure. To witness one parent ruthlessly lash out, killing the other...

"Danica?" Luke's bright green eyes held concern. "Are you okay?"

"Yes. Fine." She gave herself a mental shake. As a cop, she knew her childhood could have been worse. She'd survived and thrived in her role within the PNK9 unit. "Looks like Greg isn't too busy. Let's have a chat about those guest lists."

Luke nodded, his gaze still concerned, but readily strolled to the front desk. Caden squirmed in his arms, his eyes fixated on Hutch. The kid was a cutie, that was for sure.

It almost made her think about her own biological clock, but she thrust that thought firmly aside. No way she was going down that path. Her parenting skills were nonexistent.

"Greg, I need you to run a list of all the guests that have stayed here over the past two months," Luke said.

Greg's somber gaze shifted to her. "Does this have something to do with Stacey's death?"

"Honestly? I'm not sure." She couldn't give him details about her investigation, but having his cooperation would help. She smiled encouragingly. "I can tell you that my goal is to cover every possible angle to find the truth."

Greg blew out a breath. "Sure, I guess I can give that to you. You're the police, right?"

She nodded. "I am the police, but I can get a search warrant if that helps." Taking shortcuts wasn't her usual approach, but she couldn't deny feeling a deep sense of urgency. What if the kidnapper attempted to strike again? Or if one of the other staff members at the lodge ended up injured or worse?

And there was still the slim possibility that the attempted kidnapping was somehow related to Stacey's murder.

"Okay," Greg said. "I think Stacey would want that, too." He turned toward his computer and began working the keyboard. Minutes later, she could hear the printer spitting out pages. "Here you go. If you need more information, let me know."

"Thanks so much. Oh, one more thing. Did you see Vera the cook or any of the staff heading outside earlier today?"

"No, should I have?" Greg looked confused. "I know one of the guests went to the kitchen to talk to Vera about a recipe, so I know she was here. I didn't see anyone else, though."

"Okay, thanks." She took the two slips of paper and quickly looked at them. Not only had Greg provided the guest list, but he'd included their home addresses, too.

Many of the guests came from outside the state of Washington. She glanced up at Luke. "You've been here how long?"

"Roughly twelve weeks." He shifted Caden to his other arm. "Surprisingly, the army cut through the red tape of my compassionate discharge quicker than I had hoped. Stacey was sweet enough to pick up Caden from Seattle, so I came straight here to the lodge once released from the army."

She nodded, then turned back to Greg. "I'm sorry, but would you run this report going back one more month? It's probably overkill, but I'd rather have the information now."

"Of course." Greg didn't hesitate. He tapped a few keys and then turned toward the printer. "I hope this helps."

"It will, even if only to rule people out." She folded the papers and tucked them into her pocket. Then added, "I'm supposed to check out today, but is there a way to stay an extra couple of days?"

"Let me see." Greg worked the keyboard again. "I have guests coming in later today for your suite. I can put you in one of the rooms that haven't been repaired yet."

"Hold on a minute." Luke moved a few steps away from the desk, indicating she should follow. "Will you and Hutch consider staying in my suite? I have a spare room, there are three total and I'm very worried about Caden's safety."

She hesitated, then realized he was right. If she and Hutch were to keep them safe, they needed to be close by. And looking into his troubled gaze, she knew he was solely focused on Caden. "Okay, it's a plan."

"Thank you." He gestured and they walked toward the front desk. "Go ahead and check out. We'll get your stuff moved before Eve needs to clean the suite."

"Speaking of Eve, I'd still like to talk to her." Danica mentally reviewed the list of staff she had yet to talk to. But in her mind, the lodge's housekeeper was at the top, having been off sick the day before.

"Eve isn't here today, she's still sick, but her daughter, Marie is coming in to help in her absence," Greg informed them.

Sick? Or had the woman just tried to kidnap Caden? As she handed over her credit card to pay for the room she was vacating, she considered taking a ride to Eve Getty's house to check on her.

Rhonda Fern and Eve Getty. Maybe between the two of them, she'd be able to nail down and arrest the woman responsible sooner than later.

Surprisingly, she had to stifle a flash of disappointment at knowing her time with Luke and Caden would soon be over.

Telling herself to get over it wasn't easy. Yet she didn't have a choice. While she was primarily stationed at Mount Rainier National Park, she often had to move around to the other national parks to help her teammates.

Based on her experience with her parents' awful marriage, she'd avoided anything resembling a relationship and wasn't about to change that approach now.

No matter how attractive Luke was, especially when he cared for his adorable son.

A wave of relief hit hard once he'd helped Danica move her things from her suite to his spare bedroom. Asking for help wasn't easy—he'd forced himself to ignore the embarrassment at asking her to stay with him. Thankfully, Danica was the ultimate professional.

Once he'd held his own on the battlefield, wielding a rifle while caring for injured soldiers, but civilian life, especially being a ready-made father, was something completely outside his wheelhouse.

Caden's safety was all that mattered. Not his ego.

Plus, he needed to focus on his sister's funeral arrangements.

Once Danica was settled, he turned to her. "We should grab something for lunch. We can eat downstairs if you like, or head into Ashford. They have a nice family-friendly restaurant there."

She glanced at Hutch, who was stretched out in front of Caden. The little boy fascinated with the dog, babbling nonstop, still saying what sounded like doggy.

"Both Eve Getty and Rhonda Fern have addresses in Ashford, so heading there would be good." She hesitated, then added, "Although some restaurants aren't open to having dogs inside."

That surprised him. "I'd think a police dog would have special dispensation."

"Sometimes his K-9 vest helps, but not always." She shrugged. "I'm game to give Ashford a try."

"Great." He grabbed the diaper bag and began stuffing it with supplies. He'd learned the hard way to take everything he might need if he were stranded for six days in a snowstorm. Because if he didn't, he'd absolutely need the one thing he'd forgotten.

The image of Stacey smiling flashed into his mind, bringing a profound sadness underscored with regret. It hurt to know how he'd missed spending more time with her. Getting to know her better after his ten years of being in the service.

Now it was too late.

A thumping noise followed by a wail drew him from his self-recriminating thoughts. He turned to see Caden had crawled forward, hitting his head on the leg of the table.

"Hey, now, it's okay, big guy." To his surprise, Danica hurried over to pick him up. "You're fine."

"Doggy," Caden whimpered, rubbing at his eyes with chubby fists.

Danica turned to face him. "I can't figure out if he's upset with Hutch or wants the dog to comfort him?"

"Your guess is as good as mine," he admitted. He took a moment to double-check that he had what he needed, or what he thought he'd need, then crossed over to take his son from her arms. "Thanks."

"Anytime." Danica's voice sounded breathless. For a long moment their gazes caught and held. A tingle of awareness slid down his spine, but the connection was broken when she abruptly turned away. "Come, Hutch."

He wondered if he imagined their brief, shared moment, then thrust it from his mind. *Stay focused,* he warned himself. This wasn't a social outing. They were getting food and using the trip to figure out who might be responsible for trying to kidnap Caden.

And the person who'd murdered his sister.

The large shepherd scrambled to his feet and came to stand at her side. The dog's nose lifted toward Caden, and of course his son attempted to reach for the animal.

"I'd like to take my SUV again," Danica said. "It's specially outfitted for Hutch's safety."

"Sure." He went over to the stroller, then hesitated. "There's a car seat in my car if you don't want me to use the stroller."

"It's okay." She smiled and gestured toward her partner. "I think Hutch will remember the scent associated with the name I've given it."

He noticed she was careful not to say Blue, so he didn't, either. He took a moment to get Caden bundled in his one-piece snowsuit, then tucked him into the stroller. Soon they were out the door and in the elevator.

Danica and Hutch remained on high alert as they walked through the lobby. Outside, dark clouds made it look later than it was. He didn't mind snow—it was a welcome relief from the sandbox that was Iraq, but now that he had a baby, he didn't relish the idea of being stuck in a blizzard.

Funny how a guy's entire attitude toward life changed

on a dime after having a child. He was still getting used to thinking about someone other than himself.

Maybe that's part of the reason he'd rushed into marriage with Annette. He'd been sick of being alone. His buddies all had wives back home, making him realize something was missing from his life.

Unfortunately, things hadn't worked out the way he'd hoped. Not that marriage itself was a problem, but he and Annette hadn't known each other well enough to get married. Her giving birth to Caden ten months later only made things worse. She'd resented his time away, then began bragging about meeting someone else. Someone who was there for her when he wasn't.

To this day he was thankful Caden hadn't been in the car with Annette the night of the crash.

"I'd like to drive past the fired waitress's house and the housekeeper's place." Danica's comment interrupted his thoughts.

"That's fine." He pushed the stroller toward her SUV. While she got Hutch settled, he disassembled it so that he could secure Caden's car seat in the back.

After a solid five minutes, they were on their way. Danica had programmed Eve Getty's and Rhonda Fern's addresses into her dashboard's GPS system. "They're not that far from each other," she observed.

"Ashford isn't that big," he agreed. "Most of the people living there support the tourist business in one form or another."

"I can imagine." She glanced at him. "What are you going to do once the danger is over?"

"I'm not sure. I have the funeral to arrange, and after that?" He shrugged. "I guess it depends on Stacey's business partner, Eli. No matter what his plans are, either buying out her portion of the business or selling entirely, nothing will happen overnight. The estate will take time to settle."

She nodded thoughtfully. "Makes it difficult for you to make plans for your future."

"I've been focused on learning to be a dad," he admitted. "There's been a lot to do, and now that Stacey is gone…" He didn't finish.

It hit hard that he was truly alone in the world now. Except for Caden.

They rode in silence until they reached Ashford. Danica slowed the SUV, watching the screen. "Eve's house isn't too far off Main Street."

"What's your strategy?" He glanced at her. "If she's sick, she may not answer the door."

"I'd like to talk to her, but I think I'll use Hutch's nose as a screening test first."

"Sounds reasonable." He glanced back to where Caden was beginning to fuss. "He'll need to eat soon."

"I'll be quick." She flashed a guilty glance at her rearview mirror. "We can hold off swinging by Rhonda Fern's place until after lunch."

Five minutes later she pulled her SUV off to the side of the road next to a small white clapboard house. Danica swiftly exited the vehicle and released the back for Hutch.

"Seek! Seek Blue!" she commanded the K-9. She slammed the back door, then allowed Hutch to take the lead.

"Doggy," Caden wailed.

"The doggy will be back soon." He rummaged through the diaper bag, finding a small packet of dry cereal. "Do you want some cereal?" he asked, handing a couple pieces to his son.

Caden happily took the small O-shaped cereal bits and stuffed them into his mouth. He gave his son a few more, watching as Danica and Hutch made their way up the driveway. Hutch sniffed all around, but as far as he could tell, the dog didn't alert.

Danica knocked at the door, then stood waiting. When there was no response, she turned and headed back to the SUV.

"Doggy." Caden's voice was muffled with cereal. Luke winced when he realized there were crumbs everywhere.

"Hutch didn't seem to pick up the scent," Danica said as she slid behind the wheel. She smiled when she saw part of a round O stuck to Caden's lips. "I think we'd better get some real food, huh?"

"I'll clean up the mess," he began, but she brushed him off.

"Don't worry, it's fine." Her brow furrowed as she pulled away from the housekeeper's house. "I can't help thinking it's possible Hutch didn't really alert on the stroller scent near the kitchen door. He's a great K-9, but he never tried to track a scent from something like a stroller handle, especially one that was only held briefly and by a possibly gloved hand." She sighed. "Maybe I'm asking too much of him."

"Well, it can't hurt to try, right?"

"Right." Her tone lacked confidence. "Let's head to the restaurant."

They found the family-friendly restaurant on Main Street. As he was getting Caden's car seat unbuckled,

Luke glanced up at the dark clouds. He hoped the snow would hold off a bit longer.

"I'm sure we have some time yet before the snow hits," Danica said, guessing his thoughts. She put Hutch on leash then led the way up to the restaurant.

"Table for two adults and a high chair for the baby," he said to the hostess. "Oh, and this is Hutch. He's a K-9 officer."

"He's beautiful, but if he causes any trouble, you'll be asked to leave," the woman warned.

"He won't," Danica said with a smile. "He's better trained than most humans."

The hostess burst out laughing. "I believe it!" She led the way to a four-top table, grabbing a tall plastic high chair along the way for Caden.

They quickly gave their order. The snow outside was coming down now, and he sensed Danica didn't want to linger any longer than necessary. He gave his son a bottle to tide him over as they waited for their meals.

Thankfully, the place wasn't too busy, so it didn't take long. He was about to dig into his roast beef sandwich when Danica bowed her head to say grace.

"Lord, we thank You for this wonderful food," she whispered. "And we ask You to keep all of us, especially Caden, safe in Your care."

"Amen," he murmured, grateful she'd included his son. "I guess I'm out of practice. That was nice, thanks."

Her cheeks turned an adorable shade of pink. "You're welcome."

This wasn't their first meal together, but being at a restaurant created a new sense of intimacy. One that didn't exist, he reminded himself sternly. After taking a bite of his own food, he quickly spooned some baby

Shielding the Baby

food into Caden's mouth. This was the way he ate meals now—some for him, some for Caden.

"Hey, it's starting to snow." Danica frowned. "The storm wasn't due until later, but we should probably head back to the lodge now, rather than going to find Rhonda Fern."

He hesitated, then nodded in agreement. "As much as I'd like to know who tried to snatch Caden, it makes sense to head back."

By the time they'd finished eating, bundled Caden up and left the restaurant, there was two inches of snow covering the SUV already. He realized they'd likely get more than the predicted four to six inches if it kept up.

After securing Caden inside his car seat, he and Danica brushed off the snow. Soon they were on the road.

The snow was coming down thick, with the wind making it even harder to see. Danica took it slow, and the four-wheel drive helped keep them on the road without difficulty.

A truck came around a curve in the road, going way too fast for the wintry conditions. The truck swerved into their lane. Danica turned the steering wheel to avoid the collision. The truck missed them, but the SUV slid sideways on the road, heading straight for the ditch.

The seat belt tightened painfully across his chest as the vehicle came to an abrupt stop. He quickly turned in his seat to make sure Caden was okay.

The baby was fine, and so was Hutch. But he couldn't be sure about the SUV.

Looking over at Danica, he could see her knuckles were white on the steering wheel. "That idiot," she whispered. "We might have been killed."

"I know." Things could be worse, but from where he

was sitting? Being stranded in a snowstorm with a nine-month-old baby was not good.

They needed to get out of the ditch and back on the road as soon as possible.

SIX

Uncurling her fingers from the steering wheel, Danica blew out a breath and glanced at Luke. "Hopefully we didn't sustain any damage, but I'll need to check out the vehicle to be sure."

She shut off the engine to preserve their fuel if they ended up stuck there for a while, but he placed a hand on her arm. "Let me." He shoved his door open before she could protest. "If there's no damage, I might be able to push us out."

Even with four-wheel drive, getting out of the ditch wouldn't be easy. The snow was still coming down hard, adding to the already precarious conditions.

In her estimation, they were roughly two miles from the lodge. Close enough that they could walk if needed, although she worried about doing that with Caden.

A pickup truck rumbled past, seemingly too close for comfort. They needed to get out of here before someone else slid off the road, ramming into them.

She started the engine, using her front and rear wipers to clear the accumulating snow. Luke moved toward the back and bent to examine the wheels. She hadn't been going very fast when the guy had swerved into her lane. Praying the axel hadn't bent or broken, she waited for Luke to return.

He opened the passenger side door but didn't get in. "Everything looks good. The tires are in good shape. Let's see if we can get out of here."

She nodded. "I'm ready when you are."

He flashed a reassuring smile and shut the door. When he'd taken up a position in the back, she put the SUV in four-wheel drive. She tapped briefly on the gas, causing the vehicle to rock back and forth. Then she pressed the accelerator harder, trying climb up and out of the ditch.

Luke pushed from the back but had to jump out of the way when the car slid backward. If this didn't work, she could try to put on the set of chains she always carried, but they would be difficult to place with the way the snow was accumulating.

She mentally berated herself for not putting the chains on the tires back at the restaurant. To be honest, she hadn't even thought of using them with only two inches of snow and a two-mile ride. Stupid to underestimate the April snowstorm.

They went through the same rocking routine again, and this time she hit the gas a little harder. The rear wheels spun for a moment in the snow, but then Luke shoved hard and the vehicle made it up and over the edge of the ditch.

Success! She drove about fifty feet just to be sure that she was on the road before stopping for Luke. He jogged up to meet her.

"Thanks, Luke," she said as he climbed in, his dark hair covered with snow. "You were great."

"Nah, that was a team effort." He managed a smile as

she slowly accelerated, putting the ditch behind them. "Can't believe how much snow we've gotten already, though."

She explained about the chains, then grimaced. "Normally the four-wheel drive works well enough."

"We would have been fine if that driver hadn't been so reckless," he agreed. Luke turned in his seat to look at Caden. The baby was happily babbling and shaking a plastic key ring rattle. "I'm just glad we got out of there."

"Me, too." She kept her speed slow and steady as she headed down the highway. The wind kicked up, making it even more difficult to tell where the edge of the road was located.

It seemed to take forever to reach the lodge. The way the rustic building was blanketed in fresh snow made it look like a picture postcard.

Pretty, as long as you didn't have to drive in it, she thought grimly. And the worst thing about the unexpected snowstorm was the way it derailed the investigation into her two top suspects in the attempted kidnapping of Caden—and possibly in the murders of Stacey and Jonas. She'd really wanted to talk to each of them in person.

Looking into a suspect's eyes, watching how they answered questions, was important, but in the meantime, she could still use her computer to dig into their backgrounds.

It was better than nothing.

After pulling into the parking lot, she unclenched her fingers and shifted the SUV into Park. Then she shut down the engine and turned to Luke. "Do you need help with Caden?"

"No, I can handle him and the diaper bag." He shrugged. "I'll come back for the stroller."

"I'll grab it," she offered. "Hutch will be fine—he loves snow."

Together they hauled everything they needed into the lodge. Hutch ran and jumped into snowbanks along the way, shaking himself to get rid of the excess snow before diving into another one. Caden giggled at the dog's antics.

It made her smile, even as tiny warning bells jangled in her head. This oddly domestic scene wasn't for real. She and Luke weren't a couple. She wouldn't be here at all if not for Caden being in danger.

They entered the lobby, taking a moment to stamp snow from their feet and to bask in the warmth radiating from the fire. She put the stroller together, taking longer than Luke as she figured out how it worked. Hutch shook himself again, sending droplets of water flying everywhere.

"Well, that was fun," Luke said dryly as he connected Caden's car seat to the stroller. "If Caden was older, we could build a snowman."

"Just think of how much fun he'll have next winter," she said with a chuckle as they headed toward the elevator. "I don't mind snow, but times like this, it makes my job ten times more difficult."

His expression sobered. "Yeah, I wish you could have interviewed Eve Getty and Rhonda Fern."

"I'll keep working the case," she promised. If one of the women had a grudge against Stacey, she might have killed her, but why go after Caden, too? Just to get revenge on Luke because he was Stacey's brother? The puzzle pieces weren't quite fitting together.

When they reached the third floor, Luke accessed the suite, then stood by to let her in.

"Make yourself at home. I need to get Caden down for his nap."

"Will do." She found a towel to use on Hutch, then changed out of her wet things. Minutes later, she had her computer open and connected to the lodge internet. Hutch stretched out at her feet.

The connection wasn't as strong as she'd have liked, probably due in part to the storm. And being so far away from civilization.

"Would you like some coffee?" Luke asked.

"Ah, sure. That would be great." She frowned when she realized she was watching him as he moved about the kitchen, the baby monitor tucked into his back pocket. How a guy could look tough and handsome with a baby monitor in his pocket was a mystery.

Stay focused on the task at hand, she silently admonished. After checking to make sure neither suspect had a criminal record, she dug into their DMV records.

Disappointing to note there were no black cars registered to either woman. She switched over to various social media sites but still didn't find anything.

Luke set a steaming mug of coffee next to her elbow. Hutch shifted beneath the table but didn't move away. She glanced at him, and for a moment their gazes locked. "Uh, thanks."

"You're welcome." His husky voice sent a ripple of awareness down her spine. "Find anything?"

"Not yet." She took a sip of her coffee, then nearly choked when Luke dropped into the seat beside her. She hesitated, then added, "No criminal records on either woman."

"Did you think there would be?" His expression was one of interest.

"It's best not to take anything for granted." She pushed the computer away for a minute, regarding him thoughtfully. "You mentioned Annette had an aunt in California. I need her name and address."

He shook his head. "I'm sorry, but I don't know her name or her address."

"What about when you and Annette got married? She wasn't on the wedding invite list?"

"We didn't have a big wedding." He stared into his mug for a moment.

"Then when did she mention this aunt?" Danica knew she was pushing, but if Luke hadn't met this woman, maybe she had stayed as a guest or obtained a job working here.

He lowered his coffee and leaned forward, bracing his elbows on the table. His gaze turned thoughtful. "Annette mentioned her when we decided to get married. I was willing to wait a few days to allow her aunt to come into town, but Annette brushed off the idea." He hesitated, then added, "Wanda. I believe she said, 'Wanda wouldn't want to come all this way for a simple wedding.'"

"No last name?"

"Annette's maiden name was Garth, but I don't honestly know if Wanda shared the name." He grimaced. "I hate how little I know about my own late wife. You can try searching for Wanda Garth."

"I will." She eagerly tugged the computer closer and started with the California DMV records. To her surprise, there were three Wanda Garths but only one in the right age category. "I found a sixty-two-year-old Wanda Garth in Oakland."

"That could be it." He scooted his chair so close, their shoulders brushed. "Is that her picture?"

"Yes." She glanced over. "Does she look anything like your wife?"

"Not really. Well, other than she has a widow's peak, which Annette had, too." He sat back and reached for her coffee. "But now that I see that picture, I know she's not one of our employees."

"But she could have been a guest here at some point in the last twelve weeks." She pulled the folded guest list from her pocket. Scrolling over the names and addresses, she found one couple from Oakland, California, but they had been registered under the names Ken and Lilly Smith.

An alias? It seemed a stretch, yet she couldn't discount the possibility.

"Do you remember this couple?" She tapped the paperwork.

"Ken and Lilly Smith?" He shook his head. "No, sorry. As I mentioned, I've been rather preoccupied with Caden."

She understood where he was coming from and turned her attention back to the grainy DMV photo. Now she had three suspects. This investigation was not going the way she'd planned.

The snow was still coming down fast and furious. She could only hope that by this time tomorrow, she'd have the list narrowed down to one suspect.

She needed distance, emotionally and physically, from Luke and his son. The sooner she uncovered the identity of the kidnapper and/or murderer, the better.

* * *

Having Danica and Hutch staying in his suite was more disturbing than he'd anticipated. Luke did his best to remember that the only reason the two officers were here at all was because of the attempted kidnapping.

Maybe it was the snowstorm swirling outside the large windows, obscuring the view of Mount Rainier that provided the sense of intimacy.

Caden made a murmuring sound. Luke reached for the baby monitor, anticipating he'd wake up crying.

"How long does he normally sleep?" Danica asked.

"Usually two hours." He listened intently, glad to note his son fell silent. He set the monitor on the table. "Anything less makes for a long evening."

"I'm sure." She stood and carried her coffee cup to the sink. Hutch rose and padded to her side. "Excuse me while I make a few calls."

"Sure." He finished his coffee as she stepped into the guest room for privacy.

The image of Wanda Garth was still on the computer screen. Other than the widow's peak, he didn't see any resemblance to Annette.

Yet the woman's face did seem slightly familiar.

Or maybe he was simply letting his imagination run amok. He drained his coffee and set the empty cup aside. Danica had mentioned early on that most child kidnapping cases were custody disputes. Yet he knew full well there were plenty of other reasons someone would try to snatch Caden.

Human trafficking wasn't just about teenage girls.

He forced himself not to go down that path. Imagining the worst wasn't helpful. Caden was safe. Luke would do better at protecting him, plus they had two police officers standing guard.

There was no doubt in his mind Danica and Hutch would deter another kidnapping attempt.

Deep down, though, he understood that this current feeling of safety was an illusion. The three of them, plus Hutch, couldn't stay cooped up in the suite forever.

"Thanks, Jasmin." Danica pocketed her phone as she returned to the kitchen. She then spread out the guest list Greg had provided to her on the table. Using her phone, she carefully used her scanning app on each page. "I'm sending a copy of the list to our tech expert. She's going to start by running background checks."

"I appreciate everything you're doing to find this woman." He crossed over to the table. "Do you mind if I look these over?"

"Not at all."

It didn't take him long to realize the attempt was useless. Then his gaze went back to linger on one of the names. "This lady here, Grace Kaplan?"

"What about her?"

"She's been here for two weeks, going on a third." He searched his memory. "I met her in the dining room one day. She has the same stocky build as the woman in the black coat."

"Hmm. It's interesting that she's staying here for a few weeks," Danica mused. "And in a room right below this one."

"I noticed that, too." He shrugged. "I don't want to cast guilt on the innocent, but I have to wonder why she's sticking around for so long."

"Maybe we should have dinner downstairs," Danica said. "If we see her, we can strike up a conversation."

"We can do that," he agreed. "The kitchen closes early in the off season, so we'll have to get down there by six."

"Believe it or not, I'm already hungry, so that shouldn't be a problem." Danica offered a wry smile. "Not sure why—it's not like we didn't have a great lunch."

"Getting stuck in the snow builds up an appetite," he teased. Before he could say anything more, Caden's babbling voice came through the baby monitor. It didn't take but a moment for the little boy to begin to cry. "That's my cue," he said wryly.

To his surprise, Hutch followed him into the baby's room. "What, you don't think I can handle it?" he asked the dog.

Hutch wisely didn't answer, pressing his nose between the slats of the crib. Caden had pulled himself into a standing position and when he caught sight of the K-9, he instantly stopped crying. "Doggy!"

"Yes, indeed it is." The dog seemed to distract his son better than any toy the kid owned. Luke gave up trying to get his son to call him Daddy. Working quickly, he changed Caden's diaper, then carried him into the kitchen. Hutch again followed, like a sentry on duty.

He set Caden in his walker seat so he could wash his hands and make a bottle.

"I can help," Danica offered.

"I've got it." He'd made enough bottles by now that he didn't have to read the directions. Maybe one day being a father wouldn't feel so alien. Glancing over at Caden, he had to smile at how Hutch sat next to the boy, as if it was his job to keep the boy happy and safe.

Caden jumped up and down excitedly, pushing the walker forward several inches. He moved it again, then pinched his hand between the side of the walker and the leg of the kitchen chair.

"Waaahhh!" Caden wailed.

"Oh, you poor thing." Before he could move, Danica lifted the little boy into her arms. "It's okay, you're fine."

He shook the bottle, dissolving the formula, then reached for his son. "Here, I'll take him."

Danica came over to hand him the baby. As he took Caden, he found himself gazing into Danica's light brown eyes for a long moment.

The urge to kiss her came out of nowhere. He found himself leaning in, his gaze fixed on her sweet mouth— until Caden bobbed his head, clipping him under the chin.

He took the baby and stepped back. Nice of his son to knock some sense into him.

Even Caden knew the beautiful K-9 officer was off-limits.

SEVEN

What was she doing? Danica turned toward the kitchen table, shaken by the weird awareness she felt toward Luke that was becoming more and more difficult to ignore.

Had Luke been about to kiss her?

Would she have let him?

Yes. She swallowed hard and dropped into the chair, staring blindly at her computer. Her heart was thumping harder than when she and Hutch chased after suspects.

Enough. She needed to put a hard stop to this ridiculous happy family fantasy. Yes, Caden was cute, but she wasn't interested in going down the path of having a husband and kid. If she was, she doubted Luke was ready to jump into another relationship, either. Even without the fact he was grappling with the loss of his sister, his brief marriage hadn't sounded all sunshine and roses. If Annette hadn't died, she felt certain they wouldn't have remained married.

Not that it could have been as awful as what her parents had put her through as a child. Normally she didn't dwell much on the past. After all, her experiences had made her the cop she was today.

She was so distracted by her turbulent emotions it took a few minutes for her to realize the reason she couldn't navigate between websites on her computer was because there was no internet access. With a frown, she disconnected from the Wi-Fi, then reconnected and tried again.

Still nothing.

"Great." She slapped the computer closed with more force than was necessary. She winced and glanced at Luke. He cradled Caden in one arm and held the bottle with the other. "Sorry, but it seems the internet is out."

"That happens sometimes." He didn't look concerned. "You already completed your searches anyway, right?"

"Yeah, for now."

"When Caden is finished, we'll head to the dining room."

"Sounds good. I'll feed Hutch while we wait." After filling his food and water dishes, she stared down at her phone. There was only one bar, indicating she had poor service. Jasmin was supposed to get back to her with information regarding the list of guests who'd been at the lodge recently, including the long-term guest, Grace Kaplan. And she'd also asked the specialist to find a way to determine if Wanda Garth was still in Oakland.

A long list of requests. No sense in being concerned about the lack of phone access. Jasmin would need time to get through everything. She knew she needed to have patience, which wasn't her forte.

She turned back to see Hutch had finished eating and was stretched out in front of Caden. Clearly, her partner knew it was his job to keep the little boy safe.

When Caden was finished with his bottle, they

headed down to the lobby. The small dining room was almost full, the weather obviously causing everyone to stay inside. She was glad to see so many guests—surely the extended-stay guest Grace Kaplan was among the diners.

Luke snagged an empty table. "Here, hold Caden for me, would you? I'll grab a high chair."

"No problem." She bounced the boy on her lap, with Hutch sitting beside her. Luke took his time winding through the tables and eyeing the guests on his way to the high chairs sitting along the far wall.

When he returned, he strapped Caden into the high chair, then sat across from her.

"Do you see Kaplan?" she asked in a whisper.

Luke shook his head. "I hope we didn't miss her."

"I hope not, too." She swallowed a wave of frustration and turned her attention to the menu. There was still time for Grace Kaplan to make an appearance.

Their server was a younger woman who introduced herself as Noreen. Danica watched Hutch closely for any hint of alerting, but her K-9 partner didn't seem to recognize her scent. Noreen filled their water glasses, then asked, "Are you ready to order?"

"I'll have the roasted chicken, thanks," Danica said.

"Make that two." Luke smiled. "It seems to be the most popular item on the menu, based on what I'm seeing."

"It is," Noreen agreed. "Anything for your son?"

Danica blushed when she realized Noreen had addressed the question to her, as if assuming she was Caden's mother. "Uh, Luke?"

"No, thanks." Luke shifted uncomfortably in his seat. "I brought his baby food with me."

"Okay, let me know if you need anything else." Noreen didn't seem to notice Luke's attempt to indicate he was Caden's only parent.

Danica sipped her water as Luke pulled out a jar of baby food. Caden slammed his hands on the tray of the high chair, making the small bits of dry cereal dance around.

"Easy there," Luke cautioned. "Here you go." He spooned some green mushy stuff into Caden's mouth. Surprisingly, the boy ate it.

"I hate to tell you, but that looks disgusting."

"I'm aware, but don't let Caden know," Luke said with a wink. "He happens to like his vegetables."

A woman entered the dining room, glancing around curiously before taking a seat. Danica reached over to pat Luke's arm. "New arrival. Is that her?"

He swiped excess mushed veggies from Caden's mouth, then looked over. "Yep."

Danica slowly stood, giving Hutch the hand signal to come. The large shepherd eagerly crawled out from beneath the table to stand beside her. "Seek. Seek Blue," she commanded.

Her K-9 obediently lowered his nose to the floor. She wasn't sure this would work; the scent hadn't been that strong on the stroller to start with, and she hadn't had the opportunity to reinforce the scent with Hutch now.

Yet he seemed to know what he was searching for. He moved around the tables but didn't go anywhere near the woman who'd taken a seat at the empty table catty-corner from them.

Hutch went all the way back to the doorway near the kitchen, where he sat and looked up at her expectantly.

"Good boy," she praised, taking the tattered bunny

from her pocket and handing it to him. Normally she made more of a game out of it, but there were too many people in the dining room for that.

Instead, she led him into the lobby, where he had more space to run.

She played with him for several moments before gently taking the stuffed bunny back. "Good boy," she praised again as she went back to sit in the dining room.

Hutch sat beside Caden, nudging the little boy's legs with his nose.

"Doggy," Caden said gleefully. The jar of green mush was nearly finished, and she was impressed at how the little boy enjoyed his food.

"I guess she's not our kidnapper, huh?" Luke asked in a low voice.

"I don't think so. At least, not according to Hutch." Grace Kaplan didn't seem to notice them sitting there, her attention on the menu. Was she ignoring them on purpose, to avoid drawing attention?

Most people at least glanced curiously at Hutch; he was too big to be ignored. And almost everyone else in the dining room had smiled at Caden.

"I guess we can cross her off the list, then." Luke shrugged. "Better to eliminate suspects, right?"

"Yes." That much was true. One less suspect to worry about was helpful.

Yet as she glanced at Grace Kaplan, she was struck anew by how much the woman's rectangle-shaped stature resembled the lady who'd tried to take Caden. And according to Luke, Grace Kaplan owned a black coat.

A wave of uncertainty hit hard. She'd never used the handle of a stroller held only briefly by a perp—who had probably worn gloves—as a scent source before.

Was she asking too much? Had Hutch really tracked and located the scent of the kidnapper by the kitchen?

Or had her partner fixated on something else entirely?

Luke tried not to show his disappointment that Grace Kaplan wasn't the kidnapper.

Not that he'd expected finding the woman to be easy. But still, he'd had high hopes that Hutch would head straight over to sit beside her.

Their meals arrived, the scent of roasted chicken making his mouth water. But he knew by now that Danica would want to say grace, so he folded his hands and bowed his head.

"Lord, we thank You for this wonderful food, and for keeping us safe today," she said in a low voice. "Amen."

"Amen," he murmured. It had been a while since he'd sought peace from prayer. Maybe too long.

The conversation lagged as they enjoyed their meals. He appreciated the ability to come down here to eat rather than cooking.

Yet he knew staying here at the lodge wasn't a long-term plan. Even less so now that Stacey was gone.

He was a bit surprised he hadn't heard from Eli Ballard yet. If for no other reason than to discuss the future of the Stark Lodge business.

"This is amazing," Danica gushed. "Best chicken I've ever had."

"Agreed." He smiled as Caden leaned over the side of the high chair as if reaching toward Hutch. He gently guided the boy's hand aside. "I was just thinking how nice it was not to cook."

"Ditto on that. My specialty is mac and cheese out of a box," she teased.

"Mine is frozen pizza," he shot back.

They laughed, but then his smile faded as he thought of his sister. "I really need to figure out what the next steps are with Stacey's portion of the business."

"There's plenty of time for that." Danica's gaze held compassion. "You've been through a lot over these past two days."

Two days that seemed like a lifetime.

"I need to plan Stacey's funeral," he said, trying to keep his voice steady. "I'm thinking of having her cremated and spreading her ashes in the park. She really loved it there."

"That sounds nice," Danica agreed.

He managed a lopsided smile. "Thanks. I know my sister is in a better place, with God, yet I'm going to miss her."

"I believe that, too, Luke." Danica reached over to touch his arm.

He nodded, then said, "I must admit, I've been waiting to hear from Eli Ballard. But he could just as easily be waiting to hear from me."

"I don't have a lot of experience with wills and estates, but I doubt things move very fast, especially when the legal system is involved."

Danica was right, so he let the matter drop. He felt certain Eli was grieving over Stacey's death, as much as Luke was. After all, Eli and Stacey had been partners for the past several years. Eli had probably been closer to Stacey than Luke had, except for the past few months.

Caden slammed his hands on the high chair tray again, pulling him from his thoughts. He couldn't go back and change the past, no matter how much he wanted to.

All he could do was focus on the future.

"Ready?" he asked as Noreen dropped off their bill.

"Yes," Danica agreed. She put some cash on the table to pay for her share of the meal.

He did the same, then used a wet wipe to clean up his son's messy hands and face. He carried the boy in his arms, waiting for Danica and Hutch to move forward.

"I'll need to take Hutch out soon," she said as they waited for the elevator.

"No problem." Once they were back inside the room, he noticed the snow had finally stopped.

Danica donned her coat, hat and boots before clipping Hutch's leash to his collar. "I won't be long."

"I'm sure we'll be fine." He wasn't worried—it wasn't likely the kidnapper would brave the elements to make another attempt to grab Caden tonight.

He set the boy down on a baby quilt to let him play, athough now that he was crawling, he knew the boy wouldn't stay put for long. He checked his phone, but there was only one bar of service because of the storm, so he shoved it back in his pocket.

He'd call Eli Ballard tomorrow. It was time to pull himself together and to think about his future. He'd miss Stacey, but he also had a son who needed him. His sister would want him to take care of Caden.

With skills as a soldier and medic, he had options. Once he'd anticipated getting a job at a local hospital after he'd figured out a viable daycare situation for Caden. Sticking around the Ashford area hadn't been a part of his long-term plan.

But now he had the future of the three Stark Lodges

to consider. Not that he'd been interested in co-owning and running them.

Happy are thy men, happy are these thy servants, which stand continually before thee, and that hear thy wisdom.

The Bible passage flashed into his mind. He'd learned about God and faith while overseas and knew everything happened for a reason. Their pastor had often relayed how God was leading them down His chosen path.

A concept he'd grappled with after his marriage to Annette had gone wrong.

Yet there was no doubt that he'd been feeling at a loss as he'd coped with instant fatherhood. Now, he had to acknowledge that maybe his path forward included helping to manage Stacey's business in the wake of her passing.

Caden managed to crawl across the floor toward Hutch's water dish. "No," he said sternly, scooping the little boy off the floor and putting him back on the blanket. "That's not a toy."

His face crumpled, and he began to wail. The door of the suite opened, revealing Danica and Hutch. The dog instantly came over to press his nose against Caden as if to reassure the boy he was fine.

Luke lifted Caden to his shoulder, trying to soothe him. He met Danica's concerned gaze and shrugged. "He's upset because I wouldn't let him play in Hutch's water dish."

"Aw, maybe he's tired." She took off her coat and boots. "The snow stopped, but there's a good eight inches covering the ground. Hopefully the plows will clear the roads by morning."

"You plan to head back into Ashford tomorrow?"

She nodded. "Hopefully Eve will come in to work, but I'd still like to talk to Rhonda Fern."

Caden continued to fuss, even though he bounced the boy up and down in his arms.

"Do you need help?" Danica asked.

He would have loved nothing more than to hand the baby over, but he was Caden's father, and Danica wouldn't always be around to help him out. He managed a tense smile. "No, thanks."

He swayed from side to side, but Caden's wails only grew louder. He'd experienced this from the little boy before—it seemed he often had a crabby time after dinner.

"Here, let me try." Danica held out her arms. "You look like you could use a break."

"I'm fine," he protested. But Danica took the baby anyway and began to walk around the suite. Hutch followed at her side, staring up at the baby as if he wanted to help, too.

His chest tightened as he watched Danica speak softly to his son, telling Caden that he had to be a good boy for his daddy.

After a couple of minutes, the baby stopped fussing. Danica carefully sat on the sofa. Hutch pressed his nose against Caden's chubby arm.

"Thank you," he said in a low voice. "You certainly seem to have a way with babies."

"Oh, I'm not sure about that," she said, keeping her tone soft, too. "Caden is the only baby I've been around."

"Really?" She'd seemed so natural. "Must be your motherly instincts, then."

Her expression turned serious, and she slowly shook her head. "I hope I don't have any motherly instincts."

He frowned. "Why not?"

She avoided his direct gaze for a long moment before finally looking up. "My parents used to fight. A lot."

"Okay." He wasn't sure why that meant she didn't have motherly instincts. "A lot of parents argue."

"True. But it's not often they beat on each other." Her gaze dropped back down to look at Caden's peaceful face. His large eyes were beginning to drift closed, as if he'd worn himself out.

"I'm sorry to hear that." He came over to sit beside her on the sofa. "I hope they didn't hit you, too."

She shrugged. "Sometimes. But that wasn't the worst part. My father always struck first, but then one day my mother decided to fight back in a big way. She flung herself at my father, striking his chest with her fists. My dad never used weapons before, but that time, he did. He grabbed a fireplace poker and swung it at her head like a baseball bat. The force was enough to kill her."

He stared in horror. "Oh, Danica. I'm so sorry. No child should have to witness such a terrible tragedy."

"Yeah, well, no eleven-year-old child should have to testify in court against her own father, either," she murmured.

He longed to draw her into his arms, but since Caden was falling asleep on her lap, he had to be satisfied with simply draping his arm across her shoulders. "I'm sure your father didn't mean to kill your mother."

"Oh, I'm pretty sure he did. They threatened to kill each other often, so I wasn't surprised when they came to blows." She raised her weary gaze to his. "I tried to convince my mother to leave, but she wouldn't. Then she was dead. A really amazing female cop responded to the scene, and it's because of her that I decided to go into law enforcement."

"I'm glad." He was glad to hear that someone had helped her. "But you must realize that you're different from your parents."

"Am I?" She shrugged. "I share their DNA, which means I'll never risk having a family of my own."

"Avoiding a family isn't the answer," he protested.

"It is for me." She carefully slid Caden from her lap onto his. "Good night."

Holding his son, he watched her take Hutch into the guest room. He could only imagine how awful it had been for her to go through something so difficult.

But as he gazed into Caden's sweet face, he was sad to realize she was missing out on something precious.

A child of her own.

EIGHT

Why on earth had she told Luke her darkest secret? Even her teammates didn't know the nitty-gritty details about her childhood. Oh, they knew she'd grown up in the foster system, but not *why*.

Her parents had hardly been role models. Mostly her father, though. Yet she still blamed her mother for not having the strength to leave him.

After her mother's death, her father had been arrested and charged with manslaughter. Her father's lawyer had claimed he'd killed her mother in self-defense, because she'd come after him, hitting him with her fists. Which was partially true. But only because her father had struck her mother first. As a result of her father's not-guilty plea, Danica had been forced to testify. She'd been eleven, scared to death but determined to be honest.

Sitting in front of the judge and the jury, explaining about the abuse her mother had suffered, had been the most difficult thing she'd ever done. She'd steadfastly refused to meet her father's angry eyes, instinctively knowing that if he didn't go to jail, he'd find a way to make her pay.

The judge and jury must have believed her and maybe had seen the truth in her father's eyes as they found him guilty. She'd been in a temporary foster home but then had been placed into a permanent home.

And really, she was one of the more fortunate kids. Her foster family had been decent. They'd treated her very well. Better than her own parents had, that was for sure.

Danica washed her face, then stared at her reflection in the mirror. Losing her parents, one to death, the other to jail, had happened years ago. There was no reason to dredge it up again now.

Turning away, she padded toward the bed. Hutch was lying on the floor, watching her.

Her love of dogs had come from her work with the humane society. She'd volunteered there for several years, knowing she couldn't have a dog of her own while living with the McCarthys. They had provided food, clothing and shelter, all of which she'd appreciated very much. But they hadn't wanted to add a rescue dog to the mix.

Thankfully, she'd managed to get a scholarship to attend community college to obtain her criminal justice degree. Granted, she'd worked several jobs to put herself through school, but the end result was worth the effort.

She had much to be grateful for. So why had she bothered to travel back in time?

Because of Caden.

It wasn't the baby's fault he was naturally cute and adorable. But he represented everything she'd turned her back on over the past decade. At thirty years of age, she'd assumed she didn't have a biological clock. Not the way some women claimed.

Had she been wrong about that?

Giving herself a mental shake for even thinking it, she closed her eyes and tried to quiet her brain to get some sleep. According to her weather app, the following day was supposed to be nice and sunny. She needed to get back to work investigating Caden's attempted kidnapping along with the double homicide. Both cases had to be connected in some way. Hopefully, if she dug deep enough, she'd find it.

Which made her think about Colt and Sampson. Had her teammate and his K-9 partner found anything significant before the blizzard hit?

Tomorrow, she thought with a yawn as a wave of fatigue hit hard. She'd follow up with Colt and the rest of her team tomorrow.

The following morning, it seemed her weather app had been spot on. Sunlight filtered through the windows, bringing the promise of a nice day.

As always, she took care of her partner first. She could hear movement in the main living area, so she wasn't surprised to see Caden and Luke were already up.

"Good morning." She smiled and reached for her coat. "Be back in a jiff."

"Morning," Luke responded. "There's coffee when you're ready."

"Great." Shrugging into her coat, she slipped out of the suite with Hutch on leash and made sure she had doggie bags.

The temperature had begun to warm up, melting the freshly fallen snow. Hutch still enjoyed playing in the white stuff, but as soon as he'd taken care of business, she took him back inside.

Greg was working the front desk today, and he eyed Danica and Hutch curiously as they passed. Danica smiled and nodded, noting that Hutch didn't seem at all interested in the clerk.

The more she thought about the alert near the doorway of the kitchen, the less she believed Hutch had been able to track the scent from the stroller. If there was another kidnapping attempt, she hoped her partner would catch her. And if not, that he'd manage to bite off a piece of her coat or other clothing.

Back in the suite, the scent of coffee drew her to the kitchenette. She ran a self-conscious hand through her hair, wishing she'd had time to shower. "Something smells good."

"I thought it would be better to make breakfast this morning—if you like eggs, that is." Luke met her gaze over the rim of his mug. "If you'd rather go down to the dining room, that's fine, too."

"Eating here is good." She sipped her coffee, then set it aside. "Give me a few minutes to get ready."

"Take your time." He gestured toward his son. "I'll need to take care of Caden first, anyway."

"Thanks." It was funny how Luke had made Caden his priority first thing this morning, the same way she'd made Hutch hers. Luke might be relatively new to fatherhood, but he was a wonderful caretaker to his son.

It didn't take her long to shower and change into her work uniform. When she entered the kitchen, she was greeted by the aroma of eggs and toast.

"Caden is finished already?" She looked at the baby in surprise.

Luke nodded, then lifted a brow. "We're heading back to Ashford today, right?"

"Yes. But I need to check in with the rest of my team before we head out." She was hoping Jasmin had come up with something of interest on either the guests or Annette's aunt Wanda.

"Sounds good." Luke turned back to his frying pan. She took a moment to fill Hutch's food and water dishes before taking over the task of buttering toast.

Less than an hour later, they were finished eating and cleaning up the kitchen. She called her boss first.

"Fanelli," he answered with a clipped tone.

"Donovan, it's Danica. I'm afraid I don't have much of an update for you. A snowstorm blew in, preventing me from following up on a few potential leads. I'll get back at it today."

"Jasmin mentioned she's running a list of guest names for you." Their chief didn't miss anything that went on under his watch. "So far there are three who have criminal backgrounds, mostly related to small drug crimes."

"That's interesting." Using drugs didn't directly correlate to kidnapping, but it was something to follow up on. "It's possible the kidnapper is looking for a way to get money through a ransom."

"Anything is possible, but we both know if a drug addict was going to steal, they'd look for an easy mark. They don't usually go through the trouble of kidnapping a child."

"Yes, but we may have someone looking for a bigger payout. Has there been an update on the double homicide? Did anyone find the murder weapon?"

"Not yet on both counts." Donovan's tone sounded grim. "Our benefactor, Roland Evans, is concerned about the negative press. Especially since he's just gifted the unit three twelve-month-old bloodhound puppies."

Roland was the philanthropist who'd financially supported the grant for their entire team. Negative press wasn't great for their image, especially if one of their own was convicted of murder.

"We'll uncover the truth." She injected confidence in her tone.

"I know you will." Donovan paused, then added, "Keep me posted on your progress."

"Will do," she promised. Disconnecting from the call, she thought about their so-called murder witness, who'd called in using a mechanically distorted voice via a burner phone. It wouldn't be the first time a murderer had tried to disguise themselves as a witness.

Then again, there was no denying the way several lodge staff members had recognized Mara's picture. Sure, their crime scene tech could have been here just to talk to Jonas.

But what bothered her the most was the way Mara had run from the crime scene. If she were truly innocent, why not come forward to tell the rest of the team what she knew? That and not answering a call from the chief. Those were two big red flags.

Actions Mara would need to explain once they'd found her.

Her phone rang again, and she quickly answered. "Jasmin, tell me something good."

"Good morning to you, too," their tech expert teased. "I got all the way through your list and found six guests with criminal backgrounds, but only two of them are women."

"It's a place to start. Will you email that to me?"

"Already done," Jasmin said. "Oh, and I've called in a favor with the Oakland, California, PD. They're going to swing by and see if your suspect Wanda Garth is home."

"How did you manage that?" Danica asked in admiration.

"I sweet-talked them into it," Jasmin said with a chuckle. "And they were happy to help when they heard about the attempted kidnapping of a baby."

"You're awesome. Thanks for the information. I'll check out those names ASAP." Danica disconnected from the call, feeling as if she'd already made some progress in her day.

Today just might be the day she brought a kidnapper, and possible murderer, to justice.

"Danica, I'd like to stop by to see the area where Stacey was killed." Luke glanced over to where Danica stood. She was all business today in her work uniform, gun, badge and radio. He'd already bundled Caden in his blue snowsuit. "I know we have to go to Ashford first, but there should be time on the way back."

"Of course, that shouldn't be a problem." She appeared to be in a good mood, and he hoped that meant her check-in with her boss had gone well. "Are you ready to go?"

"Yep." Luke finished strapping Caden into the stroller.

They took the elevator down to the lobby. Luke noticed there were two couples who appeared to be checking out of their respective rooms. No sign of Grace Kaplan, though. He wondered how long she was planning to stay.

He'd felt certain she was the kidnapper, but after Hutch hadn't alerted on the scent, he'd decided he was wrong.

"Watch Caden a minute, would you?" He pushed the stroller in front of Danica, then went behind the front desk to speak with Greg. "Has Eve Getty showed up for work yet?"

"No." Greg frowned. "Her daughter came in again and said her mom has been really sick with the flu. I'm sure she'll be back soon. Oh, and Eli Ballard is driving down this afternoon. He wants to talk to the staff here, of course, but he also wants to chat with you, too."

"Yeah, sure. That's fine. I'm stopping by the Longmire Suspension Bridge on the way back from Ashford, but that shouldn't take long. Thanks for the update on Eve." Luke turned and hurried back over to where Danica stood with Caden and Hutch. "Eve called in sick again, but her daughter is coming in to clean. According to her daughter, Eve has a bad case of the flu. Stacey's business partner, Eli Ballard, is going to be here later today, too. He wants to talk to me as well as address the staff."

"I'm sure he's upset about Stacey and wondering about your plans for the future." Danica's expression turned thoughtful. "I'm glad he's coming in, though. I'd like to talk to him."

"Hasn't he already been interviewed?" Luke asked. He remembered hearing early on that the guy had an alibi.

"Yes, but I'd still like to talk to him for myself. Ready to go?" Danica turned and headed toward the door. He took control of Caden's stroller and followed.

This time, the trip to Ashford was quick and easy on the now-cleared roads. Their first stop was Eve Getty's house, but once again, the housekeeper didn't answer the door.

"I'm concerned about her welfare," Danica said when she returned to the SUV. "If not for her daughter claiming she's sick, I'd have the local police do a wellness check."

"I understand where you're coming from, but I'm sure her daughter would let us know if she needs help."

"I guess if she's that sick, she's probably not the kidnapper," Danica mused. "We'll stop at Rhonda Fern's place next."

The former server's home appeared a bit dilapidated. Luke wondered if the woman had tried to obtain another position, not easy since she'd been let go. It went against the grain to sit and watch as Danica let Hutch out and let him sniff around the front yard. Danica left the car running, so he opened the window a crack so he could hear at least part of the conversation.

"Seek! Seek Blue!"

The K-9 went to work, sniffing along the front of the property. Danica hung back for a few minutes, then approached the front door.

He glanced at Caden before turning back to watch. A woman wearing a ratty bathrobe opened the door, scowling when she saw Danica and Hutch, especially Danica's badge.

"What do you want?" Rhonda Fern spoke in a harsh voice, a cigarette dangling from the corner of her mouth.

"I'm Officer Danica Hayes. I'd like to ask you a few questions about your time working as a server at the Stark Lodge."

"I haven't been there since I quit two weeks ago." The woman glared at her for a long moment. "That's all

I'm going to say." Before Danica could respond, Rhonda stepped back and slammed the door.

Danica stood for a moment, then slowly turned to head back to the SUV. From what Luke could tell, Hutch hadn't alerted on the woman's scent.

"That wasn't very helpful," he said wryly.

"No kidding. Judging by the cluttered mess and the cloud of smoke that hung over the room, I'd say she hasn't been out much. My gut says to believe her. If you ask me, she hasn't gone anywhere since the day she walked away from her job."

He sighed. "I noticed Hutch didn't alert, either. I guess that's one less suspect to worry about."

"We may not want to base our decisions only on Hutch's nose," she warned. "Hutch is an amazing tracker, and even better at chasing down bad guys, but to be honest, I'm not one hundred percent sure he was able to get enough of a scent source from the stroller handle. Human scent can linger in the air, but when it comes to objects, the scent clings to skin cells. She was probably wearing gloves. Now if I had an item of her clothing, we'd be in business."

He nodded thoughtfully. It was interesting that clothing worked better. "If it looks like she hasn't left the house, she probably isn't the kidnapper. Even if she was upset about losing her job as a server, her issue would be with Stacey, not me."

"But if she needs money, she might be looking for easy cash in a ransom. And being upset with Stacey is also a motive for murder."

It was a possibility he hadn't considered. "Yeah, maybe she's responsible for the murder, but kidnapping? I don't know, it seems far more work than she's willing

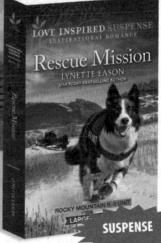

Get up to 4
FREE FABULOUS BOOKS
in your welcome box!

To thank you for being a loyal reader we'd like to send you up to 4 FREE BOOKS, absolutely free when you try the Harlequin Reader Service.

Just write "YES" on the Loyal Reader Voucher and we'll send you your welcome box with 2 free books from each series you choose plus free mystery gifts! Each welcome box is worth over $20.

Try **Love Inspired® Romance Larger-Print** and get 2 books and fall in love with inspirational romances that take you on an uplifting journey of faith, forgiveness and hope.

Try **Love Inspired® Suspense Larger-Print** and get 2 books where courage and optimism unite in stories of faith and love in the face of danger.

Or **TRY BOTH** and get 2 books from each series!

Your welcome box is completely free, even the shipping! If you continue with your subscription, you can look forward to curated monthly shipments of brand-new books from your selected series, always at a discount off the cover price! Plus you can cancel any time.

So don't miss out, return your Loyal Readers Voucher today to get your Free Welcome Box.

Pam Powers

LOYAL READER
FREE BOOKS VOUCHER
WELCOME BOX

YES! I Love Reading, please send me a welcome box with up to 4 FREE BOOKS and Free Mystery Gifts from the series I select.

Just write in "YES" on the dotted line below then return this card today and we'll send your welcome box asap!

➡ YES ⬅

Which do you prefer?

☐ **Love Inspired®
Romance
Larger-Print**
122/322 IDL GRET

☐ **Love Inspired®
Suspense
Larger-Print**
107/307 IDL GRET

☐ **BOTH**
122/322 & 107/307
IDL GRE5

FIRST NAME   LAST NAME

ADDRESS

APT.#   CITY

STATE/PROV.   ZIP/POSTAL CODE

EMAIL ☐ Please check this box if you would like to receive newsletters and promotional emails from Harlequin Enterprises ULC and its affiliates. You can unsubscribe anytime.

LI/LIS-622-LR_LRV22

to do. Stacey mentioned she was late and missed many shifts. I remember her as not being very motivated."

"True." Danica sighed. "This case is murky, that's for sure."

"Now what? Is there anything else we need from Ashford?"

She reached for her phone. "Hold on, I need to check a few things." She swiped at the screen for several minutes. "As I mentioned, Jasmin, our technical expert, has found several guests with criminal backgrounds. Unfortunately, none of them live in this area. Which makes sense, I guess." She set the phone aside.

"Can we head to the Longmire Suspension Bridge now?" He couldn't really say why he wanted to see the area where Stacey had died. It wasn't logical, yet he was anxious to go anyway.

"Yes, of course." Her expression was full of empathy. "The Nisqually park entrance isn't far. I'm sure the snow has covered much of the area, though. I hope you're not expecting too much."

"I'm not." Maybe this was a useless endeavor, but he was still glad they were going. Once he had the exact location centered in his mind, he could go back when the weather was nicer, to leave flowers and find a good place to spread her ashes.

Maybe wildflowers would be best, since he wasn't sure what she'd favored. Stacey hadn't seemed like the kind of woman who'd want red roses, but wildflowers of various shapes, sizes and colors? In his mind, that seemed to reflect his sister's laid-back and carefree attitude toward life.

A life that had been stolen far too soon.

He remembered what Stacey had said about her new

boyfriend, Jonas Digby. About how he was a Christian, like Luke. He hoped that meant Stacey had found her faith, too.

And shamefully realized he needed to mend his own relationship with God. Glancing at Danica, he was struck by how well she lived her faith, despite the horror of her upbringing.

His heart ached for the girl who'd not only witnessed her mother being brutally murdered but who had gone on to testify against her father in a court of law.

She had become a strong woman, but one who still had walls around her heart. He reminded himself that he wasn't interested in a relationship, anyway. He'd rushed into one relationship with Annette—he wasn't about to repeat that mistake.

Up ahead he saw the tall wooden sign indicating they were entering Mount Rainier National Park. The bright sun along with the mild temperatures was doing its work melting the snow they'd gotten yesterday.

"The bridge is about five miles ahead."

"Thanks." He had been to the park in the past, but not lately. When the tall suspension bridge came into view, he felt his chest tighten.

Was that the last thing Stacey had seen before she'd died?

Surprisingly, there were a few small groups of people in the area. He frowned. Reporters? Or tourists? April wasn't the peak season to come here, from what Stacey had mentioned.

Danica pulled off the road behind several other cars. "Do you want to get closer?"

"Yeah." He slid from the car, then went through the process of getting Caden's stroller together. Danica released Hutch, and together they walked toward the suspension bridge.

"She was found about here," Danica said in a soft voice. "Digby was beside her."

He stared at the ground, imaging the scene in his mind. It was probably good the snow had covered the blood. He stood silently for a moment, then abruptly turned. "Danica, I—"

The sharp retort of a gunshot cut him off. He dropped his body over Caden's stroller, as people scattered in all directions.

"Luke, take cover!" Danica shouted.

For a moment he was back in Iraq, with gunfire raining all around him. Then the sandy dunes were gone, and he was back among the snow-covered foliage of Mount Rainier park, instinctively running with the stroller to a cluster of trees.

After serving his country for the past ten years, he'd never imagined he'd be targeted by gunfire on US soil.

NINE

Pulling her weapon, Danica swept her gaze over the general area where the gunfire had come from. Seeing nothing helpful, she rushed toward Luke and Caden. "Are you okay?"

"I think so." His gaze was eerily calm, despite the acute danger. He appeared in full soldier mode. "Did you see the shooter?"

"No." She reached for her radio. "This is Officer Hayes. We have a shooter near the Longmire Suspension Bridge. Backup requested, over."

"This is Colt. Sampson and I can be there in ten."

"Roger that." She was glad her teammate was nearby. She rested her hand on Hutch's head as she scoured the area for anything amiss.

Their witnesses were running toward their vehicles. She wanted to stop them but didn't move in case the shooter was still out there.

"The gunfire came from the west," Luke said in a low voice. "I think I heard a ping as the bullet hit the metal upright of the suspension bridge. I couldn't see anything more because I was huddled over Caden's stroller."

"I agree the shot came from the west." It was just two days ago that she and Colt had run from gunfire at this exact same location. The first incident had been related to the double homicide, but today?

This was all about Luke.

Luke had been standing near the upright of the bridge, not far from where the bullet had struck the bridge. There wasn't a doubt in her mind that he'd been the target.

From the kidnapper? Or was this the original shooter who'd killed Stacey and Jonas? If they were the same person, why return to get rid of Luke? The attacker had first come after Luke with a baseball bat—to disable him to the point that she could grab the baby and run? Or had she intended to kill him? If the kidnapper was only after the baby, why shoot at Luke now? Danica had more questions than answers.

This case was growing more convoluted by the minute.

She rested her hand on Hutch's head; his nose was up, and he was sniffing the air intently. Sending him after the gunman wasn't an option—she refused to put her partner in jeopardy.

But she also wanted to find the shooter.

Colt's SUV careened up the road, coming to a halt near the walkway leading to the bridge. "Stay here, Luke. Colt and I are going to clear the scene."

Luke gave a curt nod in agreement, keeping his body strategically positioned to cover his son.

"Come, Hutch." Danica eased from cover, moving toward Colt. Her teammate had already released the back of his SUV to allow Sampson to emerge.

"You sure did go to an extreme to get my attention,"

Colt teased. But then his smile faded. "I was here yesterday morning, before the blizzard. This entire area
was quiet, and Sampson didn't find anything useful."

"I'm sure the crime scene techs finished up their efforts before the snowstorm, too." She glanced around in
frustration. "There hasn't been any more gunfire. Let's
see if we can find a trace of the shooter."

"I'm in," Colt agreed.

"I need to get Luke and Caden in the SUV." She gestured with her hand. "We believe the shot came from
the west, so we'll spread out and head that way."

Colt simply nodded, then turned to head into the
thick brush. Even though spring hadn't quite sprung,
thanks to the cooler temps and snow, there were so
many trees it made it difficult to see.

A fact the shooter had obviously used to their favor.

She jogged back to where Luke and Caden waited.
"Let's get you both to the SUV."

Luke hesitated. "Not sure having Caden in the back
seat is a good idea. Someone could fire at him through
the window. We may be better off waiting here within
the cover of these trees."

She hesitated, noting the logic in his thought process. "Okay, sit tight. We're going to see if we can find
the shooter."

Luke nodded, but she could tell by the frustration in-
termixed with longing reflected in his green eyes that
he was more accustomed to being the one taking action,
rather than sitting on the sidelines. His army training
kept him calm and focused.

"Call me if you see anything unusual."

"Count on it," Luke agreed.

She smiled, then turned. "Come, Hutch."

As she headed west, she could see Colt and Sampson up ahead. She moved several yards away, to cover more ground.

The fresh snow, even though it was fast melting in the sunshine, helped. When she stumbled across a footprint, she stopped to take a quick picture, using her own boot to help provide context. The print was larger than hers by at least two sizes. A small man, or a larger woman? Maybe. The way it was located in the middle of the foliage made her think it could be the shooter and not simply one of the park visitors.

She pointed to the footprint, encouraging Hutch to sniff it. "This is Red. Red. Seek Red."

Hutch sniffed the ground, then lifted his nose to the air to find the scent cone. She'd used a new name because she couldn't say for certain that the shooter was the woman in the long black coat that she'd already named Blue.

Not that a woman couldn't wield a handgun or rifle. Especially in this part of the country, most women could hold their own. Yet she couldn't discount the possibility that there was more than one person involved in these attempts.

Shooting at Luke had taken this to the next level. Not only did someone want Caden, but that same person would kill Luke to accomplish their mission. Or they were trying to get rid of Luke because he was Stacey's brother.

First the assault in the hallway, then the attempted kidnapping and now gunfire just barely missing Luke. The perp was escalating. And confusing in their approach. One possibility was that these attempts were all related to getting the lodges. If so, then Eli Ballard was in danger, too.

Hutch moved faster up the embankment, pushing through the brush and dislodging bits of snow along the way. She could see he was following the path of the footprints, which came to a stop near a large tree. Hutch sniffed along the ground, then sat and looked up at her.

"Good boy!" She tossed the stuffed bunny in the air for him, then examined the base of the tree more closely. There were several overlapping footprints here, as if the shooter had shifted positions frequently.

She reached for her radio. "Colt? I think I found the spot where the perp took the shot."

"Roger that. We haven't seen anything. What's your location?" Colt asked.

Using her compass, she gave him the coordinates. "I haven't found any brass yet."

"A smart shooter always picks up their brass," Colt drawled.

"I know." Although the attention to detail bothered her. The first two attempts against Luke and Caden had been a bit sloppy, crimes of opportunity.

Now suddenly an expert marksman was taking shots at him?

Colt and Sampson joined her, and they fanned out a bit to search for the shell casing.

But found nothing.

"The footprints head off in the opposite direction," Colt noted.

"Yeah, toward the road." She shrugged. "I'll have Hutch continue to follow the scent, but I'm not hopeful we'll find anything."

"You never know," Colt pointed out. "Let's go."

"Seek Red, Hutch. Seek Red!"

Upon her command, Hutch went to work. They could have followed the footprints regardless, but she wanted to cement the scent of Red in Hutch's mind. The spaces between the footprints were wider, as if the perp had run off.

The trail ended at the road, almost a mile from where she and Colt had left their SUVs. She took a moment to check the other side of the road, just to be sure the perp hadn't kept going on foot, but the snow in that area was undisturbed.

"Nothing along the side of the road, either," Colt said, picking up on her theory. "Shooter must have had a vehicle nearby."

"Yep." She sighed. "At least we can be reasonably sure the danger is over."

"For now," Colt agreed.

They turned and ran lightly back to the Longmire Suspension Bridge. When they arrived, Luke had Caden in his arms, walking back and forth and jiggling the little boy.

"That took longer than I thought," she said with an apologetic tone. "We found the location where the shooter was standing, but it appears he or she left. The trail ended at the road."

"What size footprint?" Luke asked.

She pulled out her phone to show him the screen. He stared at it for a long moment.

"Could be from the woman in the black coat," he said.

"I agree." She'd had the same thought herself. "But we have to consider she may have an accomplice."

"Let's talk to the few witnesses who stuck around," Colt said.

"Sounds good." Danica and Colt spoke to the few people who hadn't taken off. While they'd all agreed about hearing the gunfire, no one had seen anyone with a rifle.

"Do you need anything else from me?" Colt asked when they'd finished. "Chief wants me to follow up on another issue."

"No, thanks. We'll head back to the lodge as soon as the park ranger CSI team is finished."

Colt flashed a smile. "Sampson and I spent the night there because of the snowstorm, thanks to a last-minute cancellation. Nice place."

"It is." For some reason she felt self-conscious about staying in Luke's suite. Not that he hadn't been anything but professional.

If you didn't count the almost kiss.

"Come, Sampson." Colt called his K-9 partner and headed over to the SUV.

Grabbing Caden's stroller, she followed Luke to her SUV. "I feel bad your time here was cut short."

Luke paused in the act of taking apart the stroller, glancing toward the bridge. "I'm fine. I wouldn't have come at all if I'd known the kidnapper was tracking me."

"Yeah, about that." She frowned. "I didn't notice a car following us. How did the kidnapper know you were coming here?"

"I did mention it to Greg," he admitted. "Only because he let me know Eli Ballard was on his way and I wanted to assure him I would be back in time to meet with him."

She stared at him thoughtfully. "Either Greg is involved or he mentioned your plans to someone else."

"There were guests at the desk who may have overheard, too," he said. "But yeah, it's a little concerning."

"We'll find out more when we return." She used the key fob to open the back crate area for Hutch. "I'd like to know who Greg spoke to."

Luke finished buckling Caden in the car seat, storing the stroller on the floor. "Keep in mind, the lodge staff tend to be close-knit. Greg could have mentioned it in passing to one person who could have spread the word. I'm sure they're anxious to know what their future holds, too. My meeting with Eli would be big news for all of them."

She blew out a breath. Luke was right. Who Greg spoke to probably didn't matter.

Yet this entire incident had her believing a staff member or a current guest was involved.

Hopefully Hutch could help sniff out the perp.

Someone at the lodge, or close to the staff, had tried to kill him.

The sobering realization made him consider packing up and hitting the road. The first two attempts against him had been serious enough, but this?

He didn't like knowing that if the shooter's aim had been just a little better, he'd be dead.

Leaving Caden an orphan.

The little boy would end up in foster care. Much the way Danica had, unless Annette's aunt Wanda took Caden in. "Did you ever hear back on whether Wanda Garth was still in Oakland?"

"Jasmin has the Oakland PD checking in on her

today," she said. "I'm sure she'll let me know as soon as she hears back from them."

He nodded, although the news wasn't helpful. Hearing Danica's story about losing her parents, one to death and the other to prison, brought a new level of concern about Caden's future.

He really needed to know, one way or the other. If Annette's aunt Wanda wasn't involved in these kidnapping attempts, he'd need to set up a meeting with the woman. If anything happened to him and Wanda seemed like a good person, he would want Annette's aunt to be involved in his son's care.

If she was willing.

Please, Lord, keep Caden safe!

Those moments he'd crouched in the brush with Caden, he'd earnestly prayed for grace and safety. And while his relationship with God had been shaky, he'd felt a renewed strength at opening his heart to the Lord.

Something he should have done earlier. Thanks in part to Danica's faith, along with his current dangerous situation, he was slowly finding his way back.

"What time was Eli Ballard supposed to come in?" Danica's question interrupted his thoughts.

"Early afternoon." He glanced at his watch. The shooting at the Longmire bridge had taken a chunk of time out of their morning. It was 11:20 now.

"Good, that gives me some time to follow up with Jasmin, see if she has anything new," Danica said. "Even though a former guest seems unlikely as the suspect based on this current attack, I need to at least have her check them out."

He understood where she was coming from—ticking

off every possible box on a mental checklist was how the army operated as well.

When they arrived at the lodge, Danica surprised him by pulling up to the roundabout at the front door. "Better to let you out here. I'll park and then meet you inside the lobby."

"Thanks." He appreciated the extra layer of concern. As always, it took him a few minutes to get everything together, including Caden himself, before heading inside.

A tall man stood near the front desk. It only took a moment for Luke to recognize Eli Ballard. He'd met his sister's close friend and business partner twice before, but only briefly as the two lodge owners would get together specifically to discuss business. Yet Eli was clearly upset as he spoke to Greg, no doubt about Stacey's murder.

Interesting that the guy had come earlier than expected. Luke couldn't help but wonder if he'd done that on purpose to catch the staff off guard.

His army sergeants had often used surprise tactics to make sure the troops were toeing the line. Maybe Eli had suspected the workers were slacking in Stacey's absence.

He pushed Caden's stroller forward to meet him. "Hi, Eli. Nice of you to stop in."

The man turned toward him. "Oh, Luke, I'm sorry I couldn't come sooner." His gaze was full of sorrow. "I've been sick over the news of Stacey's passing. She was such a sweet woman. This has all been so horrible."

"Yes, it has." He squelched a flash of guilt over the thought that Eli had been closer to Stacey the past few years than he had. "I'm sorry for your loss, too."

"It's been a terrible shock," Eli agreed, his eyes red and puffy from shedding tears. "Stacey and I were very close, and the staff loved her, too. I can't believe she's been murdered. Even if someone was upset about something, why resort to violence?"

He put a hand on Eli's arm. "I know, it's been difficult to comprehend." He felt bad for what Eli must be going through. "Have you spoken to the rest of the staff?"

"Yes, I've made rounds," Eli admitted. "It won't be easy, but we'll have to move forward from here."

"Luke? Is everything okay?"

He turned to see Danica and Hutch strolling toward him. She eyed Eli Ballard with curiosity. "Danica, this is Eli Ballard. Eli, this is federal officer Danica Hayes and her K-9, Hutch."

"My condolences for your loss, Mr. Ballard," Danica said, shaking his hand. "I didn't realize you'd arrived early."

"Thank you." Eli summoned a weak smile. "Please, call me Eli. I gave myself extra travel time because of the snow, but the roads were nice and clear." Eli glanced at the dog. "Hutch is a beauty."

"Thanks, but he's not a pet, he's working." Luke noticed she hadn't introduced Eli as a friend to Hutch, the way she had with him and Caden. Danica gestured toward the living area in front of the fireplace. "I'd like to chat with you, if you don't mind."

"Of course." Eli appeared to pull himself together. "Anything I can do to help, but I was hoping to talk to Luke first. Maybe you and I can hold off for a bit and then the three of us can chat over lunch?"

"That works for me." Luke raised a brow at Danica. "Is that okay with you?"

"Of course. I have some phone calls to make, anyway, and I'll take Hutch outside for that. I'll join you in a few minutes." She urged Hutch toward the door.

Luke wouldn't have minded including Danica in the conversation, as it wasn't like he had any secrets to hide. Yet he was also glad to know she'd be grilling the team's tech specialist for information.

They needed to figure out who was coming after him and his son, and why.

"Shall we?" Eli asked, gesturing toward the dining room.

"Of course." He pushed Caden's stroller, following him to a table. The place was empty, either too early for lunch guests or the nicer weather had encouraged them to head out for their meals.

It took a few minutes for Kim, the daytime server, to realize they were there. When she recognized Eli Ballard, she flushed with guilt. "Oh, sorry about that. It's been quiet for the past ninety minutes. Sometimes we take a break during those lulls."

"I completely understand," Eli assured her. "I don't begrudge you time off when things are slow. Especially not during such an emotional time."

"Thanks." Kim was flustered as she filled their water glasses. "Are you ready to order or do you need a few minutes?"

"I'd love some coffee," Eli said. "But we have another guest joining us, so we'll hold off on ordering food for now."

"What about you, Luke?"

"I'm fine with water." He'd just finished getting Caden strapped into the high chair.

After Kim finished bringing his coffee, Eli leaned forward, closed his eyes and put his head in his hands for a long moment. Then he sighed and looked up. "It's been difficult to come to grips with Stacey's passing, but I have an obligation to the staff at the lodges to move forward with business as usual." He took a sip of his coffee, then said, "At some point, I'll need to understand what your plans are for Stacey's inheritance. We both had wills drawn up when we opened the business, so I know she's passing her legacy on to you."

Luke had heard about the will from Stacey, too. He'd made his will out to include her as a guardian for Caden. "I didn't ask for it."

"No, of course not. To be honest, I can't even think about moving forward without her. At the same time, I can't let the staff live in limbo for long, either."

"That's completely understandable." Luke could tell Eli really cared for his sister. "I'm afraid I don't know anything about running hotels."

Eli nodded. "There's a learning curve, for sure. I don't need an answer now—as I said, it's not something I can even consider now. But I would ask that you let me know soon if you decide you want to take her place as half owner of the lodges or sell her share of the business."

He nodded slowly. "I will."

Eli looked over the dining room for a moment. "I'm trying to think about what Stacey would want me to do. She was just as committed to this business venture as I was. I think she'd want me to keep going, but I'm just not sure..." His voice trailed off.

"Hey, there's no rush," Luke said softly. "If I decide to sell, you'll be the first to know."

"Yeah." Eli grimaced. "I'm not even sure that buying you out is an option. I'd need financing, and, well, I don't want to think about it. This isn't the time to make long-term plans." He took another sip of his coffee. "My goal for talking to you was simply to ask that we keep the lines of communication open, Luke."

"Absolutely," Luke agreed.

Eli nodded and looked down at his coffee. Then he lifted his head and sighed heavily. "Things just won't be the same without Staccy."

"For me, either," Luke agreed. As they waited for Danica to join them, he thought about his future. His and Caden's.

It was too early to worry about selling the lodges, but the idea was stuck in his mind.

What would Stacey want?

Luke hated to admit he honestly didn't know.

TEN

While Hutch did his thing, Danica wondered about the conversation Luke was having with Eli Ballard. Not that the future of the Stark Lodges was any of her concern. Colt had mentioned Eli's alibi for the time frame of the murders had checked out. Eli had been on the phone with the manager of the Stark Lodge located near the North Cascades. A call that had been verified by obtaining phone records.

Still, she was eager to talk to Eli. He wasn't high on her list of suspects, but he did have motive. It was also possible that he might be in danger, too. She was starting to think the killer might want to take over the three Stark lodges for some reason. First eliminating Stacey and Luke, then Eli.

Plus, she hoped Eli might know more about Stacey's relationship with Jonas Digby.

One possibility they hadn't really considered was that Digby might have been the primary target, with Stacey's death being collateral damage. The theory didn't mesh with attempts against Luke, but it was still an avenue they needed to delve into.

Unless Mara Gilmore had murdered them. Running

away from the crime scene and disappearing—and not answering calls—was not helping their newest crime scene tech clear her name.

No, she wasn't buying it. The sketchy witness made it difficult to believe Mara had killed two people. Donovan had told them to keep an open mind. If not Mara, then who? According to Jasmin, neither Stacey nor Jonas had any criminal history.

But that didn't mean Jonas hadn't gotten mixed up in something dangerous. He may have been heading down a criminal path, only to end up murdered before he could get caught.

Pulling out her phone, she called Jasmin. "Hey, it's Danica. Have you heard from the Oakland PD about Wanda Garth?"

"Not yet, sorry."

She sighed but didn't push. The Oakland police would make ongoing crimes their priority, not a quick check on a citizen.

"I've been busy, but I promise that if I don't hear by early afternoon, I'll call them back," Jasmin said, misinterpreting her silence.

"That's fine. There are several reasons they may have been delayed," she assured her. "I know you did a background check on Jonas Digby, but has anyone looked into his close friends and associates? Donovan mentioned doing that, but I figured he'd delegate to someone from the team."

"Yeah, I did look at some basics. Let me refresh my memory." Danica could hear Jasmin clacking on the keyboard. "Oh yes, his brother is a cop in Seattle."

"What was Digby's job?"

"He's an adventure guide for Mount Rainier National

Park. Apparently, he did many long overnight camping and hiking trips, even in the winter. From what I know so far, he came back two weeks ago from a hike up the side of the mountain."

"That's interesting." Luke said Stacey mentioned how Jonas often traveled. Now she understood why. "We should find out if he has other close friends or maybe repeat customers to find out more about him."

"I've been running his credit card information, and he has a website, too. It will take time to go through his list of clients and all his credit card purchases."

She could only imagine. "I understand. Have we uncovered anything else as far as murder suspects go?"

"No." There was a slight hesitation in Jasmin's voice as she added, "There's some dissention among the team related to Mara's guilt."

"Innocent until proven guilty, though, right?"

"Right," Jasmin agreed.

"I'll check in with Donovan later, but let me know if you hear from the Oakland PD."

"You'll be my first call," Jasmin promised.

"Thanks again." Danica ended the call. "Come, Hutch."

Her furry partner bounded toward her. She clipped his leash and walked back inside the lodge. Without hesitation, she headed directly for Eli and Luke's table.

"I'm sorry if I kept you waiting." She dropped into a chair beside Eli. Hutch nudged Caden, making him giggle, then stretched out on the floor between her and the high chair. She'd taught Hutch to only eat food she gave him, but stray crumbs from Caden were fair game.

"No, you haven't." Eli sat back with his hands folded

on the table. His earnest gaze matched his amiable attitude. "What can I do to help?"

Before she could ask any questions, Kim came over to take their order. Danica ordered a buffalo chicken wrap, while both men stayed with hamburgers.

Luke opened a jar of baby food for Caden. Normally she wouldn't interview a suspect in front of a citizen, but technically Eli had already been interviewed by a member of her team.

This informal chat was mostly for her own benefit. Her primary goal for being at the lodge was to keep Luke and Caden safe, but since Eli Ballard was here, she couldn't let the opportunity to get more information pass by.

"Thanks for talking with me," Danica said with a smile. "I know this is a difficult time for you. I was wondering if you can give me any insight into Stacey's relationship with Jonas?"

Eli looked thoughtful. "They were seeing each other for a few months, but Jonas wasn't always around when Stacey and I talked. We often had meetings via computer, since my office is in Olympia and she was mostly stationed here in Mount Rainier. It's ninety miles away, and not easily traveled in the winter."

"I see, so you didn't know Jonas very well, then," Danica said, feeling frustrated at the lack of information. Not that it was Eli's fault.

"No, I'm afraid not. Stacey and I have been friends for a long time—that's why we went into business together. Our relationship has always been just friends, though, nothing more." Eli glanced at Luke. "What I do know is that your sister was very happy with Jonas."

"I'm glad to hear it," Luke said with a sad smile. "I

like knowing she found love and happiness, even if that joy was cut off too soon."

She reached over to rest her hand on Luke's forearm. Then regretted the impulse when Eli lifted a curious brow. Why was she having trouble keeping her relationship with Luke and Caden strictly professional?

She removed her hand and focused on Eli Ballard. "I need you to know there was a recent attempt to shoot Luke. I'm afraid you may be in danger, too, Eli."

He looked surprised by her comment. "I— Really? I hadn't thought of that. But I'm not sure why Luke and I would be in danger. The lodges are heavily mortgaged— what good would they do anyone else?"

"You don't have any enemies?" she pressed.

Eli slowly shook his head. "We did very well with the lodges, especially the first year. But then we needed to have some renovations done, which required taking out additional loans." He sighed and rubbed his chin. "Right after that, we had a month of nonstop rain, which resulted in several cancellations. It's hard to imagine anyone killing over pieces of property."

"Well, it's just one theory, but I do want you to be careful." She glanced at Luke. "We don't really understand what the true motive is here."

"The lodges are beautiful and seem to be doing really well," Luke said.

"They are," Eli agreed. "But there are several newer hotels going up that are providing stiff competition. We haven't been as fully booked in the off season as we had been."

"Really?" Danica looked interested. "Is there any animosity between your lodges and their hotels?"

"Oh, you mean related to Stacey's murder?" Eli's

eyes widened. "Yes, I should have thought of this possibility earlier. We all need tourism to survive. It could be one of the competitors thought the best way to get ahead was to eliminate the competition."

"I need names and numbers," Danica said, thrilled to have another lead.

"I'll get them to you as soon as possible," Eli promised.

They exchanged phone numbers.

"The good news is that we are fully booked for the entire summer and well into the fall," Eli added. Then his face fell. "If only Stacey was here to enjoy the fruits of her labor."

"I'm truly sorry for your loss." She glanced at Luke, who had just finished feeding Caden.

Kim brought their meals. Danica bowed her head to pray, then noticed Luke had done the same.

After a moment of silent prayer, she lifted her head and picked up her wrap. "The food has been excellent. Vera is a great cook."

"We—er, I am fortunate to have her." Eli's features filled with sadness. "Losing Stacey hasn't sunk in yet. I keep reaching for my phone to call her."

"Same for me," Luke said.

"It will take time," she agreed.

The conversation turned toward the mundane, like the recent snowstorm. When they'd finished eating, Luke stood to gather Caden's things.

"I'll be in town for the next day or two," Eli said. "Then I need to check on the lodge at the North Cascades. My goal has been to talk to the staff personally, reassure them about the future. Let me know if you want to chat further."

"Of course." She smiled. "Don't forget to send me the names of your competition."

"I won't."

She waited with Luke as he cleaned up Caden, then put him in the stroller. Eli tucked his hands in his pockets and strolled back out to the lobby.

"How did it go?" she asked in a low voice.

Luke stared after Eli's retreating figure, then shrugged. "Hard to say. He didn't want to discuss the future yet, but he did give me a lot to think about."

"I'm sure." She figured Eli would have to make some decisions about the future sooner than later. Especially if the rooms were booked for the entire summer.

Luke pushed Caden's stroller toward the elevator. "I keep trying to think about what Stacey would want. Which is rather premature, since her estate won't be settled for several months. When Annette passed away, it was easier, because we were married and didn't really have any assets other than the car. I'm sure a jointly owned business will be far more complicated."

"For sure." As a foster kid, she'd had limited experience with wills and estates. But that was okay—she'd rather work for what she had. It wasn't part of her nature to lean on others.

She'd come a long way from that scared eleven-year-old who'd been forced to testify against her father.

But she was proud of her work, her role within the Pacific Northwest K-9 Unit.

She and Hutch followed Luke and Caden inside the suite. She idly wondered if Eli would stay in the suite next door, if it was available.

Her phone rang, and she eagerly answered when she saw Jasmin's number pop up on the screen. "Did you hear from the Oakland PD?" she asked in lieu of a greeting.

"I did. Two officers went to her home earlier this morning, but she wasn't there. They decided to go back just to make sure she wasn't just running errands, and this time, they were able to speak to her. You were right, she is Annette Garth's aunt and confirmed she hadn't spoken to her niece in several years."

"Well, I guess that crosses one suspect off the list. There's no way Wanda could be in two places at one time." It was both good and bad news. She hesitated, then added, "The police didn't mention Luke or Caden, did they? I have a feeling Annette never filled her aunt in on her marriage."

"No, I asked them to keep that part quiet," Jasmin said. "But I'm happy to share the address with you if Luke wants to reach out to her."

She watched Luke swinging Caden around in his arms, making the little boy laugh. "That would be great. I have a feeling Luke will want to see her. Thanks for everything, Jasmin."

"You're welcome. Gotta run—there's another call coming in." Without further comment, the tech specialist disconnected the call.

"What's the good news?" Luke asked.

"Annette's aunt, Wanda Garth, is in Oakland. She's not the kidnapper."

Luke nodded thoughtfully. "I'm glad."

Unfortunately, the good news was also bad, because they were no closer to finding the real kidnapper.

Luke tried not to dwell on his conversation with Eli Ballard. For one thing, the poor guy was grieving his friend and business partner and hadn't wanted to rush into anything. Something Luke could appreciate. Yet he also couldn't wait too long before deciding his future, either.

There had been a lot of change over the past year and a half. Marrying Annette, having Caden, then Annette's death and his discharge from the army. Now losing Stacey when he still was getting to know his son.

Being in the military meant having a strict routine. He knew how to follow orders and what was expected of him.

This new world he'd been dropped into was nothing like being in the army.

Oh, he tried to keep Caden to a schedule—some of the baby books he'd read had recommended it. Yet it seemed as if his kid had a mind of his own.

Like now. The little boy didn't seem the least bit tired, even though he normally took a nap after lunch. He set Caden in his bouncy walker, smiling when Hutch sat in front of the boy, as if to protect him.

Danica dropped into a chair at the kitchen table. "We've eliminated two suspects today, Rhonda Fern and Wanda Garth."

"Two down and how many more to go?" he asked with a sigh.

"Too many, but we'll get there. Which reminds me, I'd like to speak to Eve Getty's daughter. What was her name? Mary? Wait, no, Marie."

He frowned. "I doubt she's going to implicate her mother in a kidnapping scheme."

"You'd be surprised—sometimes witnesses let stuff slip." She smiled. "If they were all super smart, we wouldn't end up arresting so many of them."

"I suppose that's true." Yet he still didn't see it. "What possible motive could Eve have for taking Caden or shooting at me?"

"That's a very good question. Unfortunately, I don't have an answer. The two main kidnapping motives are either personal, like one spouse taking the child from another, or for money. The latter isn't done as much these days because most kidnappers know the feds will be involved. With all the technology available these days, most kidnappers realize their ability to get away with cash is slim to none."

He knew she was right. "It's a much bigger business overseas," he admitted. "Americans are often viewed as easy, rich targets."

"That's true." She sighed. "It's hard to understand the motive here."

He looked at his son. "In my humble opinion, we are dealing with a desperate woman who sees Caden as a way to make an easy dollar. Since these attacks happened after Stacey's death, it makes me wonder if the kidnapper thinks I have inherited a bunch of money with the lodges. I'm glad you warned Eli to be careful. If the property is the motive, he's vulnerable to an attack, too."

"I know." She tapped the top of the computer absently. "The average lodge employee or guest would have no way of knowing the three lodges have significant mortgages leveraged against them."

"Exactly." That was his thought. "If the kidnapper thinks I can pay a huge ransom, she's wrong. Sure, I have a decent amount of money saved up. Until I met and married Annette, I didn't have anyone to spend my money on. For years I mostly banked my checks, especially during my long deployments."

"Try not to worry about that," she said gently. "Hutch and I are not going to let this woman get close."

"I know, and I appreciate your efforts." Having Danica and Hutch in the suite provided some comfort.

Caden began to cry. He needed a diaper change. Luke snapped his finger. "I forgot the diaper bag at the table." He swung the baby into his arms. "I'll be right back."

He was already through the door when Danica and Hutch came rushing after him.

"You shouldn't go anywhere alone," she cautioned.

"I'm pretty sure it's safe enough in the middle of the day, especially since I'm only going to the dining room." He frowned. "I won't be caught off guard again."

"Doesn't matter."

The elevator doors slid shut and in a minute opened on the lobby level. As a group they headed toward the dining room.

"I'll go get it, since Caden is making such a racket," Danica said.

"Good idea." He stayed back, partially around the corner of the entryway into the dining room with Hutch at his side. Danica went over to grab the diaper bag.

He noticed Vera hovering in the doorway between the dining room and the kitchen. She was frowning as Danica picked up the bag and carried it toward him. Danica must have felt her gaze, because she looked over and gave a little wave.

Vera's frown smoothed out, and she quickly waved back before disappearing into the kitchen.

"Here you go." Danica handed him the diaper bag.

"Thanks." He glanced around self-consciously.

"I'll—uh, take him into the men's room. I think they have a baby-changing station in there."

"Good idea. We'll wait out here," Danica agreed with a smile.

He disappeared into the restroom and deftly changed Caden's diaper, the baby suddenly smiling and cooing.

He quickly rejoined Danica and Hutch in the lobby. To his surprise, Danica was kneeling beside the large shepherd. "Seek! Seek Red."

Seek Red? He remembered how the K-9 had tracked the shooter that Danica had identified as Red, versus the Blue name she'd given to the woman in the dark coat. Just in case they were two different people.

Hutch obediently lowered his nose and began to sniff along the lobby floor. As before, Danica had taken him to the entrance as a starting point.

"You think this will work?" he asked in a low voice.

"I should have thought of it sooner," she admitted wryly. "I was distracted by Eli and the possibility he'd give us more to go on."

The beautiful tan-and-black shepherd moved all around the lobby, much like he had the day before in his search for Blue. He noticed Danica stood back, giving the dog room to work.

It only took five minutes for the shepherd to make his way around the lobby and toward the dining room. Danica exchanged an excited look with Luke as they both quickened their pace to follow him.

Hutch wove between the tables until he reached the doorway leading into the kitchen. Then the K-9 sat and looked up at Danica expectantly. The same exact way he had yesterday.

Stunned, Luke blinked in surprise. If he was reading the dog's actions correctly, Red and Blue were the same person.

The woman in the long black coat had also been the one to shoot at him near the Longmire Suspension Bridge.

ELEVEN

Danica was surprised by Hutch's alert at the same location as the previous day. If he'd picked up the scent from the stroller correctly, he was telling her that the shooter and the stroller snatcher were the same person.

She pressed the door open, only to find the scent of bleach still lingered. Not as strong as the other day, but enough that she didn't want to risk taking Hutch inside.

Still, Hutch's alert left her in a bit of a conundrum. Had one of the lodge employees slipped out long enough to get to the park and shoot at Luke? She knew Vera had been there, but maybe one of the servers? Although Hutch had not alerted near either of them, either. And he would have since they moved all around the dining room.

No, she kept coming back to the housekeeper. Eve Getty hadn't worked today. If Marie had told her mother about their plan to stop at the park on the way back to the lodge, Eve could have been waiting for them to arrive.

"I guess we're looking for one person," Luke said in a low voice.

"Yes, that seems to be the case." She thought back to

the time frame between their arrival at the park and the shooting. "The park entrance isn't far from the lodge, but how long do you think we were there before the gunfire rang out?"

"Not that long—ten to fifteen minutes at the most. It always takes extra time to put Caden's stroller together." His green eyes bore into hers. "You're wondering if there was enough time for someone to have seen us drive by, then get to the park to take the shot at me."

She nodded. "Or for someone else not working at the lodge to have done the same thing." The time frame was tight, no question about it. "I'd like to talk to Greg for a minute."

Luke followed her over to the front desk. Greg was typing something into the computer, but then looked up with a smile. "Can I help you?"

"I'd like to know who you spoke to about our plans to head to the Longmire Suspension Bridge earlier."

Greg's cheeks flushed. "I—um, mentioned it to several employees. I wanted everyone to know that Mr. Ballard was coming here to talk to us and to Mr. Stark and that Mr. Ballard would meet with the staff when Mr. Stark returned from a brief trip to the bridge. It's important that everyone be on their best behavior."

"I see." She smiled tightly. "And were you here at the desk the entire morning?"

"Yes. Why?" Greg's gaze darted between her and Luke. "Is something wrong? Did you get a complaint about me?"

"No. But someone took a shot at Luke while we were at the park," Danica said, watching the clerk's expression closely. "Do you know anything about that?"

"What? No! Of course not. That doesn't make sense.

Why would someone shoot at Luke? Is it the same person who killed Stacey?" Greg's surprise and concern seemed genuine.

"That's what we're trying to find out," Danica said.

"Oh, wow. Are we in danger?" Greg looked badly shaken. "Do you think one of our guests has a gun?"

"I don't think you or the rest of the staff are in any danger," she reassured the clerk. Even though it was likely that some of their guests carried a gun. "This appears to be a targeted attack against Luke."

The fear in Greg's eyes didn't waver. "But Luke lives here. The gunman could find him here."

"I'm a federal police officer and so is Hutch," Danica said firmly. "We're here to stay until this person is caught."

Greg finally relaxed a bit. "Yeah, okay. That's good."

"Thanks for being honest with us," Danica added. "But the next time you hear where Luke is going, don't tell anyone else, okay?"

"I won't," Greg said quickly. "I promise."

"Good." She gave the clerk one more reassuring smile before stepping away. Then stopped and turned back. "Is Marie Getty still working?"

"Yes, I think she's finishing up the last room at the end of the first floor."

"Great." She glanced at Luke. "I need a moment to chat with her."

"Okay," he agreed. Although at that moment Caden squirmed in Luke's arms, then started to cry. Luke grimaced. "He needs a nap."

"Okay, let's do this quick, then." She took Hutch and hurried down the hall to where she saw the large cleaning cart outside the last room. A pretty, dark-haired woman was pulling fresh towels off the cart. "Marie?"

"Yes, do you need something?" The young woman looked tired and crabby.

"I'd like to ask about your mother, Eve Getty."

"Why?" Her sharp question had Danica raising a brow. "She's sick. Do you think I'd be doing her job if she wasn't?"

"I stopped by the house to check in on her, but she didn't come to the door."

"Why would you do that?" Marie's dark eyes narrowed. "And she wouldn't go to the door if she's feeling poorly. She's weak, running a fever and has a terrible headache. Look, is that all? Because I need to finish this room, then go home to take care of my mom." Without waiting for Danica to respond, Marie turned away.

Caden's fussing grew louder, so she gave up trying to talk to Marie. "Come on, let's head upstairs."

Luke nodded while trying to soothe the tired baby. She followed Luke and Caden toward the elevator, Hutch at her side. She rested her hand on the shepherd's head. The dog kept looking over at Caden as if he was concerned about why he was crying.

"He'll be fine, Hutch."

Luke looked a bit haggard as they entered the suite. He took Caden straight into the bedroom to put the baby down for his nap.

Looking at Hutch, she debated the value of taking her partner around the entire property again. So far, he hadn't alerted on any of the employees. And even if he did alert on the designated scent, that alone wouldn't help her identify the person involved.

They needed something more to go on. One thing

was for sure, the woman in the long black coat must also be an avid hunter and know how to use a rifle to have taken that shot at Luke at the Longmire Suspension Bridge.

It wasn't unusual for women to be good shooters, especially out here. When you lived in the wilderness, with acres and acres of national park nearby, stumbling across wildlife was a common occurrence. During her various investigations in the area, Danica had seen large black bears, wolves and mountain lions roaming the park.

Getting caught between a mama bear and her cubs could be deadly. She'd rather take on a wolf or mountain lion than a riled-up mama bear.

She opened her laptop computer, then grimaced upon finding the battery had died. Carrying the computer to the nearest outlet, she plugged it in and forced herself to be patient.

Yet sitting around in the suite when she would rather be out investigating wasn't easy. She paced as the computer recharged.

"Caden is finally asleep," Luke said with a sigh as he joined her in the living room. "I never would have imagined one small kid could be so much work."

"You're doing a great job with him." She dropped onto the sofa beside him. "He's a healthy, happy boy."

"I hope so." A shadow of concern crossed his eyes. "When the gunfire rang out, all I could think about was protecting him. And about what would happen to Caden if I was taken out of the picture."

She understood where he was coming from. The way she'd grown up in foster care was obviously weighing on him. "Maybe it's time for you to reach out to Annette's aunt, Wanda."

"Yeah, I agree. But I hate to do that while Caden is still in danger."

"Hopefully we'll get to the bottom of this very soon."

"When Eli asked that we keep the lines of communication open about my plans after inheriting Stacey's share of the lodges, I wasn't sure what to think." He ran his hands through his hair. "I don't know anything about running a hotel. He said there's no rush to decide whether to stay or sell, but I can't help thinking this might be a good place to raise Caden."

"It's beautiful here," she agreed. "But you have time, Luke. No need to stress about it now."

"Yeah. Except for the fact that my son is in danger." He shook his head. "I never flinched at running into the line of fire when I was an army medic. If my guys needed medical help, I wasn't going to let anything stop me from being there for them. But this?" He blew out a heavy breath. "It's far worse. Caden is so vulnerable."

"I know." She reached out to grasp his arm. "But we're going to keep you both safe."

"Caden first," he said firmly. His gaze locked on hers. "I want you to promise me that if there's ever a choice between me or him, that you'll rescue Caden."

Tears pricked her eyes, as she knew he was dead serious. "I promise," she said, her voice thick with emotion. "But it's not going to come to that."

"Thank you." He wrapped his arm around her shoulders and drew her close for a brief hug. In the back of her mind, she knew this was nothing more than an expression of gratitude, but somehow, the casual embrace morphed into a sizzling awareness.

Her breath shortened as he slowly, gingerly lowered his mouth toward hers. There was plenty of time for her to stop him.

She didn't.

Instead, she clutched him close and welcomed his kiss. She'd dated a few guys over the years, but none of them made her feel like this.

Like she was something precious.

She wanted nothing more than to keep kissing Luke but knew a relationship between them was impossible. Using all her willpower, she broke off from the embrace and stood on shaky legs. "I—um, need to make some calls."

Luke looked up at her, clearly seeing through her ruse. "Should I apologize?"

"What? No." She'd never been more flustered and didn't particularly like it. "But I am here to protect you and Caden. I can't afford to be distracted. Excuse me." She turned and hurried into her room.

Distracted? She could barely string two coherent sentences together.

As much as she'd enjoyed every second of Luke's kiss, it couldn't happen again.

"Help me out here, Hutch," she said to her K-9 partner. "I don't want to make a fool of myself over this guy."

Hutch stared at her for a long moment, then stretched out at her feet.

Yeah, I know, she thought wryly. *It's probably already too late for that.*

He never should have kissed Danica. Hadn't he decided he wasn't going to be involved in another relationship? Especially with a woman he didn't know very well? Look what had happened with Annette.

Luke rose to his feet and padded into the kitchen. He opened the fridge, closed it, then sighed. Okay, he needed to get a grip. A kiss wasn't a big deal.

He'd just make sure that it didn't happen again.

Feeling at loose ends, he returned to the living room. Normally he relaxed and watched sports while Caden was napping. But he was too keyed up for that now.

Between kissing Danica and Eli's brief talk about the future of the lodges, his mind spun. There was nothing he could do about the first, but he should consider getting a lawyer to advise him on the second.

The properties were heavily mortgaged, so he'd need to understand exactly what that meant before he could figure out what to do. What happened if the business didn't succeed? Eli said they were fully booked for the season, but that didn't mean things couldn't change. Especially given the increase in competition for guests.

If they went out of business, would he have to use his personal funds to pay off debtors? Or could he walk away relatively unscathed?

He told himself there was no point in ruminating over this. It was too early to make plans. Besides, his priority was to keep Caden safe. And of course, he still needed to take the initial steps in planning for Stacey's cremation. He was more convinced than ever that spreading her ashes around Mount Rainier National Park was the right decision.

The place where his sister had found Jonas Digby and happiness.

Danica stayed in her room until Caden woke from

his nap. The baby was in a much better mood, babbling nonstop as he ate small bits of dry cereal.

"Daddy?" Luke handed his son another piece of cereal. "Can you say, daddy?"

"Bawawagoo," Caden said. The baby brightened and pointed at Hutch. "Doggy!"

He sighed. "Daddy."

Caden showed him a toothy grin. Well, the four teeth he had, anyway.

"He'll learn *daddy* soon," Danica said. "It just takes time."

"I'm sure you're right." At least, he hoped she was right.

Danica crossed over to grab her laptop. She sat at the kitchen table, looking intently at the screen.

"Did you find something?"

"Eli sent the names and contact information on the three hotels he views as competitors." She looked over at him. "It looks like we'll need to take another trip to Ashford."

"Now?" He glanced at Caden, then at the clock. "We may have some time before he gets hungry for dinner."

"Yeah, I think maybe we should wait until the morning." Then she abruptly straightened. "Wait a minute. I need that list of guests who've been here for the past three months." She clicked around on the computer, searching the scanned list of names Greg had provided, for the information she wanted.

"You think one of the competitors stayed here to see what they were up against?"

She looked at him with admiration. "Yes, how did you know?"

"I'm learning the way you think," he admitted dryly.

And he was also learning how to read her facial expressions. "That's a good idea."

It didn't take long for her shoulders to sag in defeat. "It was a good idea, but the list doesn't include any of these names."

"Maybe the competitors used a friend's or relative's name when they booked a room here?"

"Maybe." She brightened and went back to work. "I'll start checking social media pages to see if any names from the list pop up."

She was especially appealing when she went into full work mode. Luke had to force himself to turn away. Enough gawking over her—this was serious business.

"How do you feel about a frozen pizza for dinner?" he asked. "If you'd rather head down to the dining room, I understand."

"I like frozen pizza," Danica said with a smile. "And I'm fine staying in the suite for the evening. If I can find a link to one of these guests and the competition, then we can head out to chat with the respective owners tomorrow."

He was glad she had a lead on Stacey's murderer, but that wasn't much help when it came to identifying his son's kidnapper. Still, he couldn't complain. It wasn't as if she and Hutch hadn't followed up every possible clue.

From what he could tell, they'd exhausted all possible leads.

He played with Caden while Danica worked until it was time for dinner. While the pizza cooked in the oven, he fed Caden and Danica fed Hutch.

By the time they were finished, the pizza was ready. Leaving Caden on the floor to crawl and play, he set the pizza on the table, then sat beside Danica.

"I—uh, would like to say grace."

"Okay." Danica flashed a sweet smile. "I'd like that."

He bowed his head and searched for the words he hadn't used in the past few months. "Dear Lord, we thank You for this food we are about to eat. We ask that You continue to guide us on Your chosen path, and please, Lord, keep Caden safe in Your loving arms. Amen."

"Amen," Danica echoed. "That was nice, Luke."

"I know it's important to repair my relationship with God." He put a slice of pizza on her plate, then helped himself to one. "Find anything on social media?"

"Not yet, but it's a long list of guests." She took a bite of her pizza. "Yum, very good."

"For a frozen pizza," he teased.

"Hey, I'm no gourmet cook," she shot back. "And I really do happen to like frozen pizza."

"Ah, a frozen pizza connoisseur! Now that's a woman I can relate to." As soon as he said the words, he wished them back. He hadn't intended to make it sound like he was looking for her to be more than a friend or protector. Especially after that incredible kiss.

"Yep, that's me." Thankfully she didn't read too much into his comment. "And remember, my specialty is mac and cheese from a box."

When they finished eating, Danica filled the sink with soapy water to wash the dishes. "I'll take care of it." He waved her away. "Keep searching for a connection between the competition and the guest list."

"Are you sure?" She lifted a brow. "I can do both."

"I'm sure." Having her so close was already messing with his concentration.

"Okay, thanks." Danica returned to her laptop.

He listened as Caden played with his toys, occasionally saying the word *no*. Sounded like maybe his son was finally learning new words, but he would have preferred *daddy*.

After washing and drying the dishes, he went over to sit on the floor next to Caden. The little boy was up on his hands and knees rocking back and forth. At the last pediatrician's visit, the doc had warned him that Caden would be walking soon, he was already standing and moving from one piece of furniture to the next. Time to babyproof the suite.

"Luke?" Danica's voice held a note of excitement. "I found something!"

"What?" He rose to his feet to peer over her shoulder.

"Here. This is Lynda Mack. A room was booked here under her name. She's the girlfriend of Oliver Roscoe." She shifted the screen so he could see it better. "And Oliver Roscoe is the owner of the Ashford Inn and Suites, the newest hotel to open in the area."

Luke stared at the woman, then at the picture of Oliver Roscoe. It was hard to imagine the guy killing a competitor just to increase his own hotel business. In his heart, he believed that Jonas's ex, the woman seen at the lodge more than once, was responsible.

Seeking justice was important, but no matter who was guilty of cold-blooded murder, nothing would bring Stacey back.

And in that moment, he realized he didn't want to take her place in running the lodges. He wanted to put his medic skills to good use.

Better for him and his son to start over someplace new once this was over.

TWELVE

Oliver Roscoe was a great lead on the murder investigation. Danica made a quick call to Jasmin, but it went to voice mail. "Jasmin, it's Danica. I'd like whatever information you can dig up on a man named Oliver Roscoe. He owns the Ashford Inn and Suites and could be a suspect in our double homicide case. Thanks."

"I'm not convinced this Oliver guy is involved," Luke said as he crossed over to where Caden was playing. "Getting rid of Stacey doesn't mean the lodges will shut down. But if she *was* the target, why kill Jonas, too?"

"You're right, but it's a possible motive and an avenue that needs to be pursued. Especially since someone shot at you now that you'll inherit her share. And Eli could be next."

"What about that Mara woman?" Luke met her gaze head on. "Seems like she has motive and opportunity."

"Mara is still a suspect," she admitted. "Trust me, we want to bring your sister's murderer to justice."

Luke nodded, but she could see a hint of skepticism in his eyes. Caden bumped his head on the edge of the table and began to cry.

"You're fine, big guy." Luke scooped the baby into his arms. "It's okay."

Caden's crying jag didn't last long. But the way the baby rubbed at his eyes with chubby fists made her think he was getting tired.

"Here, hold on to him for a minute, would you? I'll make a bottle for him. He'll be ready for bed soon."

"Oh, ah, sure." She pushed away from the table so she could hold the little boy on her lap. Hutch followed and sat beside her.

"Doggy." Caden waved his arms.

"He sure has that word down pat," Luke said wryly.

"He'll learn other words soon." At least she assumed he would. Not that she knew much about babies. She bounced Caden up and down as he grew more and more irritable. Luke finished with the bottle, then came over to take his son. He settled in the corner of the sofa and gave his son the bottle. Caden grabbed it with both hands, as if it were his lifeline.

The boy fell asleep when the bottle was finished. Danica found herself yawning, too. It had been a long day, so she thought it would be best to get some rest.

"I'll take Hutch outside one more time, then call it a day," she whispered as Luke carried Caden toward his bedroom. "Good night."

"Good night." Luke's smile made her pulse kick up, and she told herself not to overreact.

Leaving Luke and Caden alone in the suite put her nerves on edge. Thankfully, Hutch did his thing without much coaxing. She and her partner were back in the suite within five minutes.

Her body was exhausted, but her mind kept rehashing the latest information. As always, prayer helped to settle her mind.

When Danica woke up, the darkness outside made her think it was the middle of the night. But a glance at her watch indicated it was six thirty. Peering through the window, she inwardly groaned at the dark clouds overhead. Hopefully not an indication of more snow coming their way.

She quickly rose and changed to take Hutch outside. Back in the suite, she could hear Caden babbling nonsense. There was no sign of Luke. Shedding her winter jacket, she tossed it on a chair. Deciding to let Luke sleep in, she slipped into Caden's room. The boy greeted her with a toothy smile.

She quickly changed him, made him a bottle, then fed him. The baby's blue eyes were fixated on hers, and she felt her heart give a betraying thump of longing. He was so sweet, and for the first time in her life, she couldn't help but wonder what it would be like to have a baby of her own.

Foolish thought, but one difficult to ignore.

When Caden finished his bottle, she set him in his walker. She thought about making breakfast but decided to feed Hutch first.

She mentally smacked herself when she realized the small container of dog food was empty. There was more in her SUV, so she glanced at the baby, then at her partner. Just to be on the safe side, since she knew nothing about kids, she put Caden in his stroller rather than leaving him in the walker.

"Guard. Guard Caden."

The dog stretched out in front of the stroller. She trusted Hutch to watch over the baby, and besides, if Caden cried out, Luke would awaken. Safer in the stroller than crawling around on the floor. Grabbing her jacket, she silently tiptoed out of the suite and took the side stairs all the way down to the main level.

The air outside was cold enough that she could see her breath. No snowflakes yet, which she hoped would stay away long enough for her to get some investigating done. She headed toward her SUV, used her key fob to open the back, then searched for her backup container of dog food.

If she ended up staying here much longer, she'd need to restock her supplies. Eyeing the container, she estimated she had another three days of dog food left. Since she was rummaging in the SUV, she grabbed more eco-friendly doggy bags, too, stuffing them into her pocket. Was there anything else? She didn't think so.

After turning and shutting the hatch, she caught a hint of movement near the rear corner of the lodge. A person? Or an animal? Narrowing her gaze, she moved as silently as possible to investigate.

She instinctively put her hand to her belt but grimaced when she realized she didn't have her service weapon. Stupid, but she'd only planned to be gone a few minutes at most.

Upon reaching the corner, she pressed herself against the side of the log cabin lodge, then took a quick peek around the corner. She didn't see anyone, so she took another glance, longer this time.

There were human footprints, but they didn't look fresh. Hard to say for sure, after the temperatures had warmed up yesterday.

Still, she took another moment to scan the wooded area behind the lodge. Off in the distance, she smiled when she saw a large white-tailed deer moving through the trees.

Maybe that's what had caught her attention. Satisfied there was no danger lurking nearby, she turned and went back inside the lodge, using the same side entrance she had before.

As she headed up the steps, she frowned when she noticed little puddles of water. For sure, those hadn't been there before.

The tiny hairs on the back of her neck lifted in alarm. Thankfully, Hutch was in the suite. Still, she double-timed it, taking the three flights of stairs up as fast as she could.

Using the key card, she carefully opened the door. The first thing she noticed was Hutch lying on his side, unmoving.

What in the world?

Suddenly the door was flung open and a dark shape swung something long and hard at her. The thrust of the blow was enough to knock her off balance. She fell to the ground near the elevator, just as a woman wearing black, including a ski mask over her face, rushed out of the suite, pushing Caden in the stroller.

"No!" Danica crawled forward managing to grab ahold of the stroller wheel. "Stop! Police!"

Caden began to cry. The woman released the stroller and fled, the abrupt movement catching Danica off balance. She had to hold on to the stroller enough to prevent Caden from toppling sideways and hitting the floor. Luke must have heard the commotion, because he came rushing out of the suite.

"Stay with Caden," Danica said breathlessly, dragging herself to her feet. "I'll go after her."

"No, wait. Something's wrong with Hutch." Luke put a hand on her arm. "You need to check on him. The kidnapper is either hiding and you won't easily find her anyway, or she planned her exit well and is long gone."

Letting the woman escape bothered her, but she didn't dare leave if her partner was injured. Luke took care of Caden as she rushed to kneel beside Hutch.

The shepherd was lying still, a small tranquilizer dart lying on the floor beside him.

"He's been drugged."

"Let me see." Luke knelt beside the shepherd, checking his breathing. He jumped up, grabbed his medical kit and took out his stethoscope. He wasn't a vet, but she trusted his ability to listen to Hutch's heart. He pulled the stethoscope buds from his ears. "His pulse is strong. Looks like he may have managed to get the dart dislodged, but we still need an antidote."

A flash of anger toward the woman hit hard, but she held it at bay as she made a quick call to her boss. "Donovan, Hutch has been shot with a tranquilizer dart during another attempted kidnapping—same perp—of Caden Stark. She got away again. I need our team vet to meet me in Eatonville as soon as possible. It's the closest veterinary clinic to the Stark Lodge."

"Of course." To his credit, Donovan didn't ask a lot of questions but disconnected to make the arrangements. She was sure he'd also send officers to look for the brazen woman.

Danica looked at Luke. "I need you to help me carry him to the SUV. We'll use a bedsheet as a sling, okay?"

"Good idea." Luke pulled a sheet off his bed, then helped her shift the ninety-pound dog onto it. Once Hutch was in the sling, they were able to lift him easily enough. She noticed Luke somehow managed to push the stroller holding Caden, as well.

As they hauled Hutch into the elevator and out to the SUV, Danica reverently prayed her K-9 partner would be all right.

It was all his fault. Luke fed Caden some dry cereal from the diaper bag he'd snagged upon leaving the suite as he sat in the veterinary's waiting room.

The ride to Eatonville hadn't taken long with Danica behind the wheel. Yet now that the initial emergency was over, he couldn't escape the truth. Last night, thoughts of Danica, grief over Stacey's murder and concerns about his future kept him awake until one o'clock in the morning. He hadn't slept in since being discharged from the army after Annette's death and taking care of Caden. His son never let him oversleep.

This morning, when he'd heard Hutch growl and bark, he had been slow to realize something was going on. Those long seconds had nearly cost him his son.

If Danica hadn't arrived when she had, that woman would have succeeded in taking Caden.

Now Hutch was fighting for his life after being drugged.

He should have reacted quicker. Should have immediately known his son was in danger. And Hutch, too.

What had happened to his keen soldier instincts?

He'd never felt more like a failure. Not even when he learned Annette wanted to end their marriage to be with her new boyfriend. They were both to blame for their hasty rush to the altar. This time, the blame was his alone.

The door to the exam room opened, and a weary-looking Danica came out. He jumped to his feet, searching her gaze. "How is he?"

"He's going to be okay." Her eyes were awash with tears, and she quickly swiped them away. "Not sure why I'm crying now."

He stepped forward to draw her into his arms. "I'm so sorry, Danica."

She rested her cheek against his chest for a moment before lifting her head to look up at him. "It's not your fault, Luke. This is the kidnapper's doing. I really wish I had been able to go after her."

He grimaced. "You're being kind, but I know I should have been able to react quicker. I should have known something was wrong when I heard Hutch growling and barking."

"And if I hadn't waited to refill Hutch's dog food container, she wouldn't have gotten in at all." Danica sniffled, swiped at her face again, then frowned. "Although that does make me wonder how she knew I was out of the suite in the first place. When I was at the SUV, I thought I saw movement near the back corner of the lodge, but how on earth did she know to hang out there?"

"Maybe she was waiting for you to take Hutch outside, not realizing you already had," he said thoughtfully. "Without the dog being there, she may have gotten away sooner."

"And she brought the tranquilizer gun just in case?" She blew out a breath. "Maybe. But risky."

"Honestly, the whole thing is strange. What woman carries a tranq gun around with her?"

"This one, apparently. She must have brought it to take Hutch out of the picture. And since it's likely that

Red and Blue are the same, she fired at you at the Longmire bridge," she pointed out. "Clearly, she knows her
weapons. To be honest, it doesn't surprise me that she
would have a tranq gun, not when she's living so close
to all the wildlife. It would be foolish not to be armed
in some way. Especially since hunting is illegal."

Luke nodded. She was right, but it was still unnerv-
ing. He'd thought he'd left people trying to shoot at him
behind in Iraq.

Apparently not.

"Officer Hayes?" The vet, a redhead with *Dr. Waldorf* stitched on her white lab coat, came out from the
exam room. "Hutch is beginning to wake up. He's a
large dog and didn't get the full dose, so he's already
doing better thanks to the fluid bolus I've given him.
I'd still like to keep him for at least eight hours of observation."

"I understand. Can I see him?" Danica pulled out
of his embrace to join the vet. "Thank you so much for
coming out like this, Dr. Kate."

"Hey, a helicopter ride was a fun way to start my
day," the vet said wryly.

As Danica and Dr. Waldorf went back into the exam
room, Luke slowly sank back into his seat. Caden was
happily shoving a rattle into his mouth, gnawing on it in
a way that made him think more teeth were on the way.

He dropped his head in his hands for a moment, surprised and humbled that Danica didn't blame him for
failing to protect Hutch and Caden.

The front door opened, startling him. He jumped up
and stood in front of Caden's stroller, relaxing when he
saw a woman carrying a white fluffy dog. She eyed him
warily before heading over to the desk.

"Snookie is here for her shots."

"Great, please take a seat," the receptionist said. "The tech will be with you shortly."

No threat, just another patient.

Danica returned a few minutes later. "Hutch recognized me."

"I'm glad." He pushed Caden's stroller to meet her halfway. "Are you sure about leaving him for a while?"

"Yes, I know he's in good hands with Dr. Kate." She glanced over her shoulder one last time before moving toward the door. "We need to get back to the lodge. The woman was wearing gloves and a ski mask, so I didn't ask for the national park crime scene techs to come out. But I want to check the suite anyway. We left in such a hurry, we didn't get a chance to look around. Maybe she dropped something."

"I hope so." He'd take whatever lead they could get. Once they were outside, he paused, glancing at the overcast sky. "Did you want to stop and talk to that competitor whose girlfriend booked a room at the lodge?"

"No. We need to make sure the suite is safe moving forward." Her gaze softened on Caden. "Protecting you and that little boy is the top priority."

Again, he was touched by her efforts and silently promised to do better. He'd do his best to prevent anyone from getting to his son.

From now on, Caden would sleep in Luke's room.

The trip back to the lodge took twenty minutes. As soon as they entered the lobby together, something that seemed strange without Hutch tagging along, Eli Ballard rushed forward.

"I heard something happened to your dog, Officer Hayes." The man looked distraught. "Will he be okay?"

"Yes, thanks. He'll recover without a problem." Danica lifted her chin. "Someone managed to get into Luke's suite, and I need to know who would have a master key card."

"A key is never given to anyone other than the guest," Eli insisted, his voice rising with agitation. He turned and looked at Greg behind the desk. "Do you know anything about providing anyone an extra key to Luke Stark's suite?"

"No. I can guarantee no one would give a key to anyone except Mr. Stark and Officer Hayes," Greg said, looking uncomfortable to be in the hot seat. "Everyone here knows him by name."

"Would your system track every key that was made?" Danica asked.

"Yes. Hang on." Greg went to work on the computer. After a long minute, he shook his head. "No new keys were made in the past week except for the one we provided to you, Officer."

"That may be true, but the housekeeping department has a master key," Luke pointed out.

"How often do they clean your suite?" Danica asked.

"Just once a week, and that's only for the bathroom, linens and towels. I take care of the rest of the cleaning myself."

"They haven't been in recently, though, have they?" she pressed.

"No, they generally clean my room every Monday."

"Eve Getty." Danica turned to look at Greg. "Has she reported to work today?"

"No, her daughter, Marie did." Greg's gaze bounced between Danica and Eli Ballard. "I—uh, can change the housekeeping key so that it doesn't include Mr. Stark's room."

"Do that," Eli said firmly. "And make Mr. Stark and Officer Hayes new keys as well." The lodge owner turned toward Luke. "I'm so sorry. Nothing like this has ever happened before."

He nodded, accepting the apology. This woman who'd set her sights on Caden wasn't Ballard's fault.

Greg programmed the new key cards, handing one to Luke, one to Danica and the other to Eli.

"I'll give this to Marie right now." Eli turned to find the housekeeper.

"Let's go upstairs," Danica murmured.

They crossed to the elevator and rose to the third floor. She took the key from him and opened the door. She lifted a hand, warning him to stay back for a moment as she carefully stepped inside.

Less than a minute later, she gestured for him to come in. "I don't see anything unusual, do you?"

"No." He took Caden out of his stroller and set the baby down on the blanket. Together they went into each of the three bedrooms. "She didn't dress him in his snowsuit—too much in a hurry to get away, I guess."

"I noticed." Danica took another long sweeping glance around the suite.

"I doubt the cook or servers would have easy access to a master key." He grimaced. "I hate to say it, but I think it's time to move Eve Getty to the top of the suspect list."

"I was thinking the same thing," Danica admitted. "But you mentioned Eve having arthritis that prevents her from moving too quickly. The woman who tried to take Caden ran off without a problem."

"Maybe she played up that arthritis bit to throw me off track." Luke sighed and rubbed the back of his neck. "If so, I wonder what else she lied about."

Between her absence from work and her easy access to a master key, he was convinced Eve Getty was the kidnapper.

And he wanted her arrested and tossed in jail as soon as possible.

THIRTEEN

Now that Hutch was getting the care he needed, Danica realized she was hungry. It was going on ten and they hadn't eaten breakfast.

As if reading her mind, Luke stood. "I'm famished. If we head down to the dining room now, we can still get breakfast."

"Sounds good. Just give me a minute to change." She wanted to be dressed in her full uniform, including her service weapon, from this point onward. Without Hutch's nose and protective instincts, she was the only thing standing between Caden and the kidnapper.

Ten minutes later, they were taking the elevator down to the lobby. Luke pushed Caden's stroller toward the dining room.

Keenly aware of Hutch's absence, Danica followed Luke and Caden. The dining room only had one other table in use. Luke chose a table off to the side, and she made sure to sit where she could face the open doorway.

Kim hurried over carrying a coffeepot and two mugs. "Coffee?"

"Yes, please," she and Luke said at the same time.

Danica smiled. The adrenaline rush was fading away,

leaving her weak and shaky. The kick of caffeine would be welcome. She kept her phone close, hoping to hear good news from Dr. Kate. The vet had mentioned Hutch might be discharged sooner, depending on how he fared.

Although she was happy for him to stay at the clinic for as long as necessary.

Vera, the cook, came out of the kitchen and made a beeline for their table. "Good morning, Luke and Caden. I've been so busy, there hasn't been time for me to come out and visit." She dropped a kiss on the top of Caden's head, then frowned at Luke. "I was hoping you'd bring Caden back to see me."

"I know, but it's been a little busy for us, too." Luke smiled at her. "Maybe once things calm down a bit."

"Yes, but you should know how much I look forward to being with this little guy." She rested a hand on Caden's back. "I think he's grown since I last saw him."

"Oh, I doubt that." Luke managed a wry smile. "Although he may have gained a pound or two."

"You have a way with babies," Danica said. "Do you have any children or grandchildren of your own?"

"Oh, ah…" For a moment Vera looked flustered. "No, I don't. I should get back to the kitchen," she said, changing the subject. "Luke, don't you forget to bring Caden by later to see me."

"I won't," Luke assured her.

As soon as Vera left, Kim returned to take their order. She also poured more coffee.

"I still feel terrible about Hutch," Luke said as he gave Caden dry cereal.

"Hey, he's going to be fine. Dr. Kate is an excellent vet."

"You really had her flown into town?"

"Yes. Our headquarters and training center are in Olympia. We have a mutual aid agreement with the rangers to share a helicopter. Our team is spread out over a vast area, and having access to a chopper is very helpful."

Luke regarded her thoughtfully. "How often do you have to travel?"

She shrugged. "It depends. My primary site is here near Mount Rainier, but I've had to help my teammates on occasion." She thought about how quickly Donovan had reacted to her request for support. "It's a great group to work with."

"I can imagine." Luke sat back in his seat as Kim brought their food. Then he surprised her by reaching over to take her hand. "I'd like to say grace."

She smiled and tried not to notice the tingle of awareness that danced up her arm. "I'd like that."

"Lord, we thank You for keeping Hutch and Caden safe in Your care. We are grateful for this food we are about to eat and ask that You continue to keep us all safe. Amen."

"Amen." Their fingers clung for a moment before she pulled away to pick up her fork. "Thanks, Luke."

They ate in silence for a few moments. Then Luke said, "I assumed Vera had grandkids—she's been so great with Caden."

"Some women are born with great maternal genes." She was surprised to feel those same instincts with Caden, considering she hadn't planned to have a family. "She's a nice lady and maybe a bit lonely, too. She would probably love to spend more time with your son."

"Yeah, I'll make time to visit later." Caden began to

fuss, so he reached over to pluck the boy out of his high chair, setting him on his lap.

"Doggy," Caden whined.

"He's going to miss Hutch once this is over," Luke said wryly. "I see a dog in my future."

"Hold off until he's older," she advised with a smile. "Have you given any more thought as to what you'll do when the danger is over?"

He nodded slowly. "Yes, but I keep going back and forth. One day I want to start over someplace new, using my medic skills to help care for those who are hurt. The next day I think this isn't a bad place to raise a child."

She understood his dilemma. Once the tourist season hit, he and Caden couldn't very well continue to stay in the suite. Not when they were booked solid for the summer. Although they could move into Stacey's small living quarters located in the private wing off the back of the lodge.

When they finished eating, they headed up to the suite. While Luke changed Caden, she called Donovan. "Hutch is doing better," she informed her boss.

"Glad to hear it. No idea who this kidnapper is?"

"Not yet. But I'll be looking closely at the lodge's housekeeper. I also got a lead from Eli Ballard. He mentioned recent hotels have opened, causing some competition for the lodges. One of the owners may have stayed at the lodge under his girlfriend's name. I left a message for Jasmin to check it all out." She stared out the window of her room for a moment, frowning as she realized it overlooked the parking lot. Was that a black Honda parked way in the back? From here she couldn't read the license plate, but she could tell it wasn't covered in mud. "Sorry, I have to go, I need to check on something."

"I'll ask Jasmin what she's found on the competitor. Meanwhile, keep me in the loop," the chief ordered.

"I will." She ended the call and hurried out to the main living space. "I'll be right back. I need to look at something. I hate leaving you here alone, but I should only be gone five minutes."

"We'll be fine now that the key's been reprogrammed," Luke assured her. "Although I'm thinking I need to get a gun, very soon."

It wasn't a bad idea, and something she should have considered earlier. "Hopefully we'll get this kidnapper into custody and you won't need it."

"Yeah, and I know there's a waiting period for the background check to be done. Still, I'd like to consider the possibility."

She couldn't argue, and as a soldier, she was confident Luke knew his way around firearms. Feeling alone without Hutch at her side, she left the suite, and took the side staircase all the way down. Breaking into a run, she headed toward the black sedan.

Suddenly the brake lights flashed. What in the world? The car abruptly pulled forward and began to drive away.

From this angle she couldn't make out who was behind the wheel, but her gut instincts were screaming at her to follow. She veered off toward her SUV, grabbing her radio. "Colt, do you read me?"

"Loud and clear, Danica. What's up?"

"I'm heading after a suspect. I need you and Sampson to get to the Stark Lodge ASAP to protect Luke and Caden."

"Roger that." To his credit, Colt didn't pepper her with questions. "We're roughly ten minutes away."

"Thanks." She wrenched the driver's side door open and slid behind the wheel. Seconds later, she peeled out of the parking lot, in time to catch a glimpse of the black sedan's taillights up ahead.

She hadn't lost it!

Hitting the gas, she closed the gap. Then she keyed her radio again. "Colt, I need you to call Jasmin to get an ID on a plate number. Ready? Charlie, Romeo, Alpha 779."

"Charlie, Romeo, Alpha 779," Colt repeated. "Got it."

"Good." Maybe she was overreacting—there were hundreds of black sedans in the state of Washington.

But she wasn't about to ignore a potential lead.

The car disappeared. She pushed forward, determined to find it. She passed a dark green ranch house on the right, then saw the car pull into a garage.

Yes!

Danica drove a little farther before turning around, not wanting the driver of the vehicle to notice her. Then she pulled off to the side of the road a good fifty yards away, to go the rest of the way on foot.

By the time she reached the house, the garage door was closed. There were no lights inside, either. She frowned. Had she missed the vehicle leaving? Maybe the driver had forgotten something and had only spent a few minutes there?

An employee, perhaps? Rushing home to get something she needed? Her pulse quickened as she imagined Marie leaving work for a few minutes in the middle of her housekeeping shift. Maybe she didn't live with her mother, Eve, but just went over to help care for her.

Staying low, Danica lightly ran toward the far side of the property, then dropped to her knees beside the window. Could this be Marie's house?

She took a quick peek, searching for signs of the occupant. When she didn't see anyone, she took another, longer look.

A package of baby diapers, a container of formula and baby toys were on the sofa. Did Marie have a baby? She continued searching for clues, her gaze coming to rest on a wedding photo. Expecting to see Marie posed beside her husband, a chill snaked down her spine when she realized the groom was wearing a full dress military uniform—and his handsome features were Luke's.

And the woman beside him was not Marie, but a blond-haired woman. Annette? Had to be.

She ducked back down, her heart racing. Pulling out her phone she called Luke.

"Danica? Is something wrong?"

"I'm at a house about a mile from the lodge. There are baby things inside, along with a wedding photograph of you and a blonde woman."

"Annette was blonde. But I don't understand—why would there be a picture of us at that house? I don't know anyone who lives around here."

"Good question. The address is 122 Hickory Lane." She was about to ask if Colt had gotten there yet when she sensed someone coming up behind her. She turned and tried to ward off the attack. Something long struck hard along the side of her head, even as she lifted her arm. Pain radiated thorough her head and forearm.

Then everything went dark.

"Danica!" When there was nothing but silence, he knew something was wrong. He thrust the phone in his pocket and quickly bundled Caden into his snowsuit. There wasn't a moment to waste. He grabbed Caden's diaper bag and his medical kit. Then he rushed out of the suite, hoping and praying he wasn't too late.

It took what seemed like forever to get his son buckled in his car seat. He slid behind the wheel and started the engine. Thankfully, the car started up without a problem, despite his not driving it for the past few days.

He had to take precious seconds to put the address in his phone map app. Then he drove straight to the house, wondering again why on earth his and Annette's wedding photo was out on display in this house.

It didn't make any sense. He didn't know anyone in the area, and Annette's only relative, Aunt Wanda, was in Oakland, California.

Not Ashford, Washington.

He didn't see Danica's SUV, which was concerning. As he approached the property, though, he caught a glimpse of a woman dressed in a long black coat, snow pants and ski mask pulling an unconscious figure over the ground and toward the woods.

The kidnapper had Danica!

He yanked the car to the side of the road and shoved his door open. "Hey, you! Stop! That's a police officer!"

Startled by his shout, the woman dropped Danica and ran farther into the woods. Luke debated following her, but Danica lay unmoving on the ground, and he didn't dare leave Caden unattended for that long.

Leaving him in the car at all wouldn't be easy. But it was a cool morning and he'd be fine locked inside for a few minutes. He grabbed his medical kit, locked the door and sprinted toward Danica.

Dropping to his knees beside her, he took a deep

breath and searched for a pulse. Upon feeling the steady beat of her heart, he continued his assessment.

There was a large bruise forming on her temple, so he rummaged in his kit for a pen flashlight to check her pupils for signs of a concussion. The left was ever so slightly larger than the right.

Not good. "Danica? It's Luke. Can you hear me?"

No response. Grabbing his stethoscope, he listened to her heart and lungs, then ran his hands over her arms and legs. He didn't have X-ray vision, but it didn't seem as if she had other injuries. Worried about Caden and Danica, he looped his arms beneath hers, lifted her shoulders and began to pull her toward the road.

An SUV with the same PNK9 logo as Danica's pulled over near his car. Luke didn't stop pulling Danica closer but let out a silent sigh of relief when he recognized Danica's teammate Colt, along with his bloodhound, Sampson.

"What happened?" Colt looked concerned as he rushed over. With his help, they were able to move faster over the terrain.

"I saw the kidnapper dragging her toward the woods. Set her down here and call 911."

Colt did as he requested, using his phone to contact the emergency operator. Luke listened to the request as he continued caring for Danica, keeping an eye on the SUV where his son was.

Taking her hands in his, he bent close. "Danica, can you hear me? Can you squeeze my hands?"

Danica moaned slightly, then squeezed his hands. Both of them with equal strength. He sent up a prayer of thanks, then waited for her beautiful eyes to flutter open. "Luke? What happened?"

His gut clenched. "You don't remember?"

Confusion flashed across her features, then cleared. "Yes, I saw your wedding photograph in the window of a house. Baby things, too. Then I felt someone behind me and was hit over the head. I—I think she used a baseball bat."

The same weapon she'd used against him outside the elevator. "I saw the kidnapper. She was wearing a long black coat while dragging you toward the woods."

"Did you recognize her?" Colt asked.

Luke thought for a moment. There was something familiar about her, but he'd been too far away to see her facial features clearly. "No, sorry. But if she lives here, we should be able to find her."

"The owner of this house is the kidnapper?" Colt sounded surprised.

"I think so." Danica struggled to sit up. He put a restraining hand on her shoulder.

"Easy, the ambulance will be here shortly."

"I'm okay. This is important." Her words were tough, but her pale features told him she wasn't up to par. "Help me up. I want to show you what I found through the window."

"Please don't exert yourself too much," Luke cautioned, offering his hand to help her. "Head injuries are no joke. Do you feel sick to your stomach? How is your vision? Blurry?"

"Clear vision, and only slight nausea." She leaned heavily on him for a moment. "This way."

He and Colt followed Danica to the window of the house. She gestured to it and said, "Tell me that's not your wedding photo, Luke."

A shock wave of alarm skittered over him as he

looked inside. The baby diapers were the exact same brand he had at home for Caden.

And the wedding photo was definitely of him and Annette.

"That makes no sense," Colt said with a frown.

"That photo might be probable cause for a search warrant," Danica said. "I'm going to call Donovan." She reached for her phone, then hesitated. She didn't have it. She poked around in front of the window and found the device where she must have dropped it after the assault.

"Okay, but don't get your hopes up," Colt cautioned. "One picture doesn't mean much."

"It's proof the owner of this house is obsessed with Luke, and maybe with Caden," Danica insisted. "And I saw a black Honda sedan pull into the driveway."

"Speaking of my son, I need to get him out of the car." He estimated only ten to fifteen minutes had passed since he'd rushed after Danica, but even that much was too long.

"I looked inside when I got here, and he seemed fine," Colt said. "I left a message with Jasmin, hopefully she'll get back to us, soon about who owns this place."

Luke nodded and ran to the car. Seeing his crying son filled him with distress. He quickly unlocked the door.

"I'm here, it's okay. You're fine." He unbuckled Caden and gathered him close. "Shh. You're okay."

"Da," Caden said, clear as day. The little boy clutched at his jacket as if he'd never let go.

Luke couldn't help but smile despite the seriousness of the situation. *Da* was the closest his son had gotten to calling him daddy. "Yes, Daddy's here. I love you, Caden. You're safe."

He turned and headed back to where Danica stood beside Colt.

"Donovan didn't answer," she said in a grumpy tone.

He noticed Sampson was sniffing the ground around the window and he realized what Colt was trying to do.

"You're going after her?" It was more statement than question.

"As soon as the ambulance gets here," Colt agreed.

"I can watch over Danica. Why don't you and Sampson go? Maybe she's hiding in the woods nearby, waiting for us to leave."

"I agree with Luke—go ahead and search." Danica scowled. "Donovan will hopefully get back to me about the warrant, so we're on hold until we get that. I want that woman found and prosecuted for both attempted kidnapping and assaulting a police officer."

"Okay, will do." Colt turned to his K-9 and gave the command to seek.

The bloodhound put his nose to the ground near the window, sniffing at length before he trotted across the property in the same direction the woman had dragged Danica's body. Luke was impressed by the skill of the K-9s and hoped Hutch would be released from the veterinary clinic in Eatonville very soon.

The wail of a siren indicated the ambulance was on the way. Danica didn't seem as if she cared; her face was pressed up against the window again.

Then she turned so abruptly, she nearly lost her balance. He rushed forward to put his arm around her waist, the other still holding Caden.

"I thought you weren't dizzy?"

"I'm not unless I move too fast." She leaned against him and held out her phone. She pushed a button, then another to place the call on speaker. "Jasmin, do you have a name for the owner of that black Honda sedan?"

"Yes, the owner is Alice Garth, and the address is 122 Hickory Lane."

"Wait, are you sure?" Luke asked. His heart thudded painfully against his ribs as Danica stared at him. "Alice Garth?"

"Yes, why?" Jasmin asked in confusion.

"What is it, Luke?" Danica asked.

"Alice Garth is the name of Annette's mother." He pushed the words through his hoarse throat. His grip on Caden tightened as everything suddenly made sense.

Why had his wife lied to him? Her mother wasn't dead the way she'd claimed. The woman was very much alive, living within a few miles of the Stark Lodge.

And she obviously wanted to take his son, her grandson, away from him.

Permanently.

FOURTEEN

Ignoring the throbbing pain in her head and the nausea churning in her stomach wasn't easy, but Danica did her best to concentrate on what Jasmin had told them.

The kidnapper was Caden's maternal grandmother. Was she also the one who'd killed Stacey? Maybe, but the motive was murky.

Or maybe her head injury was making it difficult to think clearly enough to understand the connection.

Luke appeared devastated by the news, and she couldn't blame him. His wife had lied to him, and that had nearly cost him his son. Why any woman would do such a thing, she had no idea.

But it didn't matter. Right now, the focus had to be on finding Alice Garth. Before she made another attempt to hurt Luke or grab Caden.

There was no Alice Garth on the lodge guest list or on staff. Which made her wonder if Eve Getty was really Alice Garth.

That would make Marie, if she was really Eve's daughter, Annette's sister. Was that even possible?

The whole thing was making her head hurt worse than ever.

"Is everything okay?" Jasmin's voice pulled her from her thoughts.

"Yes, thanks. That's helpful information." She kept her gaze on Luke. "As soon as I hear from Donovan, we'll hopefully search the house. And we'll need to put out a BOLO for Alice Garth."

"Okay. The woman doesn't have anything on social media, but I'll get a copy of her driver's license photo to you. Let me know if you need anything more from me," Jasmin said before ending the call.

The ambulance siren grew louder. She winced against the intense pain reverberating through her head and swallowed against the urge to throw up.

She may have downplayed her symptoms just a bit.

"You look pale." Luke put a hand on her arm to steady her. "Are you okay?"

"Yes." Well, she would be. It irked her to be sidelined the moment they'd gotten their first real break in the case.

"This way." Luke called the EMTs over. "I'm Luke Stark and this is Officer Danica Hayes. She was assaulted about twenty-five minutes ago and has sustained a concussion."

The EMT eyed Luke curiously. "Are you a nurse?"

"No, but I spent ten years as a medic in the army."

"Thanks for your service. If you ever need a job, the Pierce County emergency response team is short-staffed. We'd welcome someone with your experience." The EMT stepped closer to her. "Officer Hayes, will you please have a seat?"

The seat was on the gurney he and his partner had brought over. Knowing she wasn't getting away without being looked at, she reluctantly sat on the cart.

"When I last checked her pupils, the left was slightly larger than the right," Luke said. "She has a bad headache and is nauseated."

"How do you know?" she asked in weak protest.

"I can tell by the way you occasionally put a hand to your stomach." Luke stared at her. "You need to be honest about your symptoms in order for us to treat you."

"He's right," the EMT said.

"Okay, yes. I feel sick to my stomach and have a bad headache," she admitted. "But I don't have time to go to the hospital. There's work to do. The woman who assaulted me is on the loose."

"Colt and Sampson will find her. In the meantime, you're going to the hospital, end of story," Luke said firmly. "Do not fight me on this."

She wanted to stay, to be there when they got the search warrant for Alice Garth's home.

"Luke? Has her pupil size changed from the last time you checked?"

Luke stepped closer, shifting his son out of the way. He took the penlight and flashed the beam into her eyes. "Yes, the left is bigger than what I noticed before."

"We need to get her to the ER right away," the EMT said. "She needs a CT scan of her head."

"Are you sure?" Danica protested.

"Yes. Very sure." Luke turned toward the EMT. "Eatonville is the closest hospital, right?"

"Yes. The ER there can do the head scan."

Danica brightened at that news. At least she'd be close to Hutch while they checked her out.

"Please lie back on the gurney," the EMT said.

"I can't leave until Colt and Sampson return." Even

as she said the words, Luke gently pushed her backward so she was lying on the gurney.

"He's coming now," Luke told her. He and the EMT exchanged a glance. "Let's give them one minute to talk."

"Fine with me," the EMT agreed.

"Danica? You okay?" Colt jogged over to the gurney.

"She has a serious concussion and needs to get to the Eatonville emergency department," Luke said. "I take it the kidnapper got away?"

"For now, but I plan to take Sampson back out soon and we can ask the local police to chip in, too. I returned to check on you, Caden and Danica." Colt's expression was grim. "I'll take over things from here."

"I left a message for Donovan about Alice Garth. It makes sense, now that the housekeepers probably clean the dining room and kitchen area, too, which is why Hutch alerted there." She blinked and tried to focus on Colt. "You need to get that search warrant and issue the BOLO. We have to find her."

"I'll take care of it. You just concentrate on getting better."

"Okay." She gave up fighting against the trip to the ER. She closed her eyes and tried to will away the wave of nausea that hit hard.

She didn't have time for this. Alice Garth was still on the loose.

But the sad truth was, Danica was in no position to go after her.

"I'll follow you to the hospital," Luke said as the EMTs rolled her toward the ambulance.

"See you there," the EMT said as they collapsed the gurney and slid her inside.

The trip seemed to take forever, maybe because the jostling only made her headache worse. Finally, they wheeled her into the ER.

From there, she answered dozens of questions about who she was, who the president of the United States was, what day it was, etc. When the medical team had finished poking and prodding, they took her for the head scan.

Fifteen minutes later, she was back in a room with an ice pack pressed to her temple. Some thoughtful nurse shut off the agonizingly bright lights.

"Danica? You feeling okay?"

Luke's voice had her opening her eyes. He stood near her bed, with Caden in the stroller beside him. "Did you shut off the lights?"

"Yes." He reached over to take her hand. "The doc should be here soon with your CT scan results. I'm glad I could get here in time to hear them. Rest now. I'll stay close by."

"Thank you." The blessed darkness along with the coolness of the ice eased the ache in her head enough to make it more tolerable.

Somehow, she managed to doze off. When she awoke, Luke and Caden were still sitting at her bedside. Humbled by his support, she turned to face him.

"You don't need to hang out here all day."

"Yes, I do." His smile was lopsided. "I've been praying for you to feel better."

"Oh, Luke. That's the sweetest thing I've ever heard." She wasn't lying—no one had ever prayed for her. At least not that she was aware of.

"Ms. Hayes?" A short man wearing green scrubs

came into the room. "I'm Dr. James Henry. You took a rather nasty hit to your head."

"Yes, she did." Luke rose and offered his hand. "I'm a former army medic, Luke Stark. Do you have the results of her head CT?"

Dr. Henry glanced at her. "Is it okay if he hears this?"

"Yes, he's my—" She had to stop herself from saying *boyfriend*. Where had that come from? "My friend," she amended. "He helped save my life."

The doc nodded. "The good news is that your head CT is normal. Yet we need to observe you here at the hospital for the next twenty-four hours. If any of your symptoms change, we'll want to do another scan."

"Twenty-four hours?" She couldn't help sounding dismayed. "That long?"

"We can reevaluate early tomorrow morning, but yes, that's the plan for now."

"I'll make sure she stays here for as long as necessary," Luke said.

She frowned. "I don't need a babysitter."

Luke ignored her comment, but Dr. Henry cracked a smile. "The team is working on getting you transferred up to a regular room. I advise no screen time, including television."

"I don't watch much TV anyway." She let her eyelids drift shut. The darkness was a very welcome relief.

She sensed rather than heard the doctor leave. Then smiled when she heard Caden babbling.

"Is he bothering you?" Luke asked.

"Never." She gingerly turned her head and smiled. "Thanks for everything. But you really don't need to stay all night. I promise to behave. And I'm sure the chief will assign Colt and Sampson to protect you."

There was a slight hesitation, before Luke nodded. "I know. We'll see how it goes."

"Okay." Once again, she closed her eyes. And this time, she didn't fight the need for sleep.

Caring for Caden while not disturbing Danica's badly needed rest was difficult. He used everything he had in the diaper bag to keep the boy occupied.

He ended up taking Caden down to the hospital cafeteria to feed him lunch, realizing he'd need to head back to the lodge for more supplies from his suite if he was really going to stay the night at the hospital.

There was nothing wrong with Colt offering protection, but he couldn't bring himself to leave the hospital. He and Colt had spoken several times now, so they had each other's phone numbers. He called Colt again while he was grabbing a bite for lunch in the small cafeteria.

"Danica's head CT is fine, but they're going to keep her overnight for observation," he informed Colt.

"Thanks for the update. I'm here at Alice Garth's house. The place hasn't provided much by the way of information." Colt sighed. "If you're sure you're okay at the hospital for a while, I'd like to take Sampson back out to search for Alice's scent. I called Donovan, he hasn't been able to free up any other members of the team yet, but he's working on it."

"I'm fine here," he quickly assured Colt. "In fact, I'd like to stay overnight with Danica, if they'll let me."

"Even with Caden?" Doubt lingered in Colt's tone. "Are you sure about that?"

No, he wasn't sure how it would go with Caden, but he intended to try. "I don't want her to be alone."

"You care about her a lot, don't you?" Colt asked.

More than he should. It was the wrong time and place to think about how much he'd come to care for her, but he wouldn't lie. "Yes, I do. Keep in mind, she was injured because of me. Or rather, because the mother-in-law I didn't know I had tried to kidnap my son."

"Okay, hang tight at the hospital for a while. I'll check back in with you, later, okay? Rest assured we have a BOLO out on Alice Garth. Every cop in the area is looking for her."

"Thanks. Talk to you later." He ended the call and slid the phone back in his pocket.

Luke was sure he was safe here at the hospital. For one thing, Alice had disappeared into the woods, so she would have no way of knowing he was there. Even if she concluded Danica had been rushed to the closest hospital, it would be a risk for her to show up here, to find them. To try to kidnap Caden again.

He'd asked the hospital to keep Danica's information confidential for now. Just to be on the safe side. Since her assault was what had brought her in, they'd readily agreed.

The most difficult part of hanging out here would be to stay focused on watching over Danica while keeping Caden occupied.

When Caden fell asleep for his afternoon nap in the stroller, he slid back into Danica's new room on the second floor of the small hospital. He noticed she was connected to a monitor that measured the oxygen level in her blood, displaying a reassuring ninety-nine percent.

He had to admit, being surrounded by medical care and equipment was interesting. It reaffirmed his decision to put his medic training to good use, rather than to consider a business partnership with Eli Ballard.

The EMT job opening would be a good place to start. After Alice Garth had been caught and tossed in jail.

The chair in Danica's hospital room was hardly comfortable, but he was oddly content to watch her sleep. He was deeply and humbly grateful God had spared her life.

Looking at Caden, Luke knew he needed to get back to attending church on a regular basis. He wanted his son to grow up knowing and loving God.

He'd often wondered, if he and Stacey had grown up with faith, if their lives would have been different. Maybe not his—he'd always planned to join the army after high school—but for Stacey?

Possibly, but it was too late to look back over what might have been.

He focused on how Eli had mentioned Stacey's happiness with Jonas Digby. Which made him wonder if Danica's team had ever found Digby's family and/or friends.

Was it possible Alice Garth had killed Stacey? It didn't make sense unless there was more to the story. He made a mental note to ask Colt for his opinion. He had a personal reason for being invested in bringing Stacey's murderer to justice. But he trusted Danica and the rest of the K-9 team would uncover the truth.

Ninety minutes later, Caden woke from his nap. About the same time, Danica stirred and opened her eyes. For a second she looked confused, then must have realized where she was.

"You're still here?" She pushed herself up on her elbows, the ice pack he'd replaced several times sliding off toward the edge of the mattress. "Luke, you should head back to the lodge. I'm sure you could use the rest."

"I'm resting just fine here. How are you feeling?" He took the ice pack, resisting the urge to check her pupils for himself, knowing the nursing staff would be in soon to do that very thing.

"Better, actually. My headache isn't as bad, and I'm growing hungry." Using the controls, she lifted the head of the bed.

"Take it slow," he advised. "Start with broth, Popsicles and Jell-O."

"Not a fan of Popsicles." She wrinkled her nose. "But the broth sounds good."

A bit later, lunch had arrived and Danica was sipping her broth when Colt knocked lightly on the door. "Danica?"

"Come in." She smiled as Sampson began to sniff around the room. "Did you find her?"

"Not yet." Colt's expression was full of frustration. "We lost her trail near the road. My theory? She flagged someone down for a ride."

Luke could easily see how someone would stop to help an older woman who appeared in distress. "Did you find anything else at her house?"

"Nope, other than she is clearly set up for a baby." Colt glanced briefly at Caden, then at Danica. "She has a crib, changing table and all kinds of baby things."

"We need to figure out where she'd go," Danica said. "What about her driver's license photo?"

"That's why I'm here." Colt scrolled through his phone, then held it up for Luke to see. "Do you recognize this woman from the lodge?"

He stared at the image for a long moment. There was something familiar about her, but the photo was grainy, her brown hair streaked gray and pulled severely back, giving her a gaunt look. "She doesn't look like any of the staff from what I can tell."

"Are you sure she's not Eve Getty?" Danica pressed. "I think she may be the kidnapper and her daughter, Marie, is covering for her. If Luke's late wife lied about her mother being dead, she also might have lied about not having a sister. Maybe Eve and Marie are even in cahoots on the plan to take Caden."

"Donovan said the judge won't approve a warrant to search Eve Getty's house," Colt said with a sigh. "Not without a positive ID on her from this driver's license photo."

"Let me see it again," Luke said. He took Colt's phone and stared at the face for a long time. The eyes—there was something about the eyes. They reminded him of someone…but who?

The phone rang, so he handed it back to Colt. Colt answered the call, then said, "Okay, Chief, I'm in Danica's hospital room. Let me put you on speaker."

"Can you hear me?" a deep male voice asked.

"Yes, loud and clear." Colt glanced at Luke, then turned toward Danica with a raised brow. "We have Luke Stark in the room, too."

There was a brief pause, then Donovan said, "Okay, this shouldn't take too long. I mostly called to check on you, Danica. And to give you an update on your K-9 partner."

"Hutch?" Her eyes widened in fear, and Luke noticed her fingers gripped the blanket. "What's wrong? Is he okay?"

"He's fine. Dr. Kate said he's doing well clearing the drugs from his system. After learning about you needing to stay the night, she's agreed to keep Hutch, too.

We're hoping you'll be recovered enough to pick him up tomorrow morning."

"I'm doing better, Donovan. I'm sure that won't be a problem."

"I think we'll wait to hear from your doctor on that one," her boss said dryly.

"Okay." Danica smiled reluctantly. "I understand."

"Any other updates?" Colt asked. "We can ask Luke to leave the room."

"I'm going." Luke quickly pushed Caden's stroller toward the door.

It was difficult knowing he wasn't part of the team. Something he'd missed since leaving the army. His army buddies had always been there for him, and the feeling was mutual.

As he walked down the hall away from Danica's room, he had never felt quite so alone.

And knew the feeling would only get worse. Once the K-9 team had found and arrested Alice Garth for attempted kidnapping, and possibly killing Stacey and Jonas, Danica would leave him and Caden behind.

For good.

FIFTEEN

Watching Luke leave with Caden gave Danica a flash of guilt. As Stacey's brother, he had a stake in the out come of her murder investigation and deserved to be updated on their progress.

Yet she also knew Donovan wouldn't talk freely with a civilian in the room.

"No key updates, unfortunately." Donovan's voice sounded weary.

"We must consider Alice might have killed Stacey and Jonas. I'm not sure why, despite missing Luke earlier, she seems comfortable using a gun. Which reminds me, there's still no sign of the murder weapon?" Danica asked.

"Nope." Donovan paused then added, "We haven't heard anything more from our mystery witness, either. And no one has heard from Mara. Not even her brother."

Danica hadn't gotten the sense that Mara and Asher Gilmore, Mara's half brother and a fellow K-9 officer with the PNK9 unit, were particularly close. But this had to be hard on him.

"You really think we may hear from the mystery witness again?" Colt asked. "Why call in that he or she saw a dark-haired woman shoot a young couple and then be unreachable? Unless that supposed witness has something to hide."

"Agreed," Donovan said. "Especially if Mara is being set up to take the fall."

Danica exchanged a long look with Colt. "That is something to consider," she said, breaking the silence.

"How are the three bloodhound puppies that our benefactor donated to the unit?" Colt asked, changing the subject. The tragic loss of Roland Evans's wife years ago to violence in a Washington State national park had led him to form a grant that would enable the PNK9 unit to have the resources needed to bring perps to justice. Future police dogs, like bloodhounds with gifted noses, were a welcome donation from the kind man.

"Peyton Burns is working with them," Donovan said, his voice sounding more cheerful as he spoke about the unit's lead trainer. "She's getting them accustomed to the terrain in the national parks and has started some basic scent training. Roland's grandson named the three puppies Chief, Ranger and Agent."

"I'm sensing a theme," Danica said with a wry smile. There was no doubt the adorable bloodhound puppies would soon be wonderful additions to their team.

Colt's radio crackled, so he took a step back to respond. "This is Officer Maxwell."

"This is Park Ranger Jeff Burgess. We have a call about possible blood being found near the Nisqually entrance to the park. Figured you may want to check that out. Could be nothing other than an injured animal, or it could be related to your case."

"Roger that. On the way." Colt stepped forward.

"Donovan, I'm heading back to the park. Do you need anything else?"

"No. Be safe. Oh, Danica, Willow and her K-9, Star, are on her way to help fill in while you're recovering."

"I won't be off very long," she protested, but her boss wasn't buying it.

"She'll be there soon, if she's not already. Star's specialty is explosives detection, as you know, but she's cross-trained to find weapons. She may be of help finding the murder weapon while at the park. Take care and I'll check in with you tomorrow."

"Thanks." She disconnected from the call and handed the phone back to Colt. "You heard about Willow heading over?"

He nodded. "Sampson and I are going to the park now—let her know she can join us when she gets here." He turned away. "Come, Sampson. Time to work."

Alone in her room, Danica closed her eyes again. Her headache was better, but there was no denying she wasn't in top form. For the first time in the four years she'd been with the team, she was content to let Colt and Sampson take this possible clue.

She wondered where Luke and Caden were. Swinging her legs over the side of the bed, she moved over to locate her belongings the nursing staff had bundled together. After digging out her phone, she returned to her bed and was about to text him when there was a hesitant knock at the door.

"Danica?" She glanced over to see Willow and her German short-haired pointer, Star, hovering in the doorway. "Are you up for a short visit?"

"Yes, of course." She set the phone aside. "Donovan told me you were heading this way."

"Yes, he sent me to help back you up." Willow stepped farther into the room. "How are you feeling? I was horrified to hear what happened to both you and Hutch."

"I'm better, and so is Hutch. I'm hoping we'll both be released tomorrow morning." Her smile faded when she saw the dark circles under Willow's eyes. "You look as if you're not getting enough sleep."

Willow shrugged, and she avoided Danica's gaze in a way that made her wonder if there was something going on with her teammate. "I'm worried about Mara. I know she didn't kill anyone. And to be honest, I wish Donovan was working harder to clear her name."

"I understand why you're supporting her," Danica began, but Willow waved a hand.

"Come on, a mystery witness calling from a burner phone that's impossible to trace? How convenient. You have to admit, there's too much about this that isn't adding up."

That much was true, but Danica couldn't help but think Willow was giving the newest team member too much credit. "You're right. We need to consider the possibility Alice Garth is the murderer. Although I'm not sure why she felt the need to kill Stacey and Jonas."

"I know, there must be something more going on here," Willow said thoughtfully.

Another good point. "Okay, but then why did Mara take off from the scene? Two cops, her own colleagues, were standing right there! And she never answered the chief's call! No one knows where she is, Willow. She's clearly in hiding."

Willow's shoulders slumped as she tucked a strand of her long brown hair behind her ear. "I don't know why she ran and didn't answer the chief's call." Her voice was a mere whisper. "I just think there has to be more going on that we don't know about."

Danica sighed and rested back against the pillows. "Maybe you're right. At this point all we can do is to keep searching for the truth and to pray."

"I've been praying a lot these days." Willow drummed up a smile. "I should let you get some rest. Call if you need anything."

"I will." As Willow turned, she took a step back in surprise. "Oh, hi. I didn't see you standing there."

"Sorry to startle you," Luke pushed Caden's stroller into the room. "Am I interrupting?"

"Not at all," Willow said quickly as Star sniffed Caden's stroller. Was it Danica's imagination or did Willow's gaze linger on Caden? Willow had recently separated from her husband and so far had not let her personal issues impact her professional life. Yet the separation was clearly taking a toll on Willow getting enough sleep. "I was just leaving."

"Colt is at the Nisqually park entrance if you want to catch up to him," Danica said. "He's been called to investigate some blood that was found there. It's probably from an animal of some sort, but he's checking it out."

"Happy to help. Take care of yourself, Danica, and Hutch, too." Willow managed a smile, then drew Star closer as they left the room.

She waved her hand, indicating Luke should come all the way in. "I'm sorry you had to leave before."

He grimaced. "I don't like it, but I understand."

She felt certain he must have overheard some of her conversation with Willow but decided to let it go. To be honest, she couldn't blame him for eavesdropping.

If the situation was reversed, she'd have done the same thing. "I promise you'll be the first to know when we arrest whoever killed your sister."

"I believe you." Luke pushed Caden back and forth in the stroller, making the little boy giggle. "I know there's nothing that will bring Stacey back, but I would like her killer to be found and arrested."

"That's our prime objective, too," she assured him. Putting a hand to her temple, she added, "I think I'm going to get some rest. I'm feeling better overall, but my headache is lingering."

"I'll take Caden and give you some quiet time," he offered.

"No, stay." Her gaze locked on his. "I like having you here, Luke."

He blinked in surprise. "Are you sure?"

"I'm sure." She waited until he took a seat beside her bed, then closed her eyes.

For some strange reason, one she didn't dare examine too closely, having Luke and Caden nearby made all the difference in the world.

Sitting around and doing nothing wasn't easy. Luke played quietly with Caden, surprised Danica was able to sleep despite his son's babbling.

He pulled out his phone and began searching for EMT job openings. Sure enough, the Pierce County emergency rescue squad had two emergency medical technician positions posted. Being a medic didn't automatically mean he could walk into the job. He'd have to investigate further to understand what additional skills and training he'd need.

But he felt certain it wouldn't take too much time for

him to become qualified to work with the ambulance crew. And doing something to help others was important to him. He loved Caden. Having these past several weeks to bond with his son had been wonderful.

But it wasn't enough to satisfy him on a long-term basis. Just thinking about the EMT job gave him something to look forward to.

He'd need to find a babysitter for Caden, though. And while that wasn't insurmountable, it wouldn't be easy, either. Ashford was a small tourist town, and everyone worked long hours in the height of the season.

Maybe he'd have to consider relocating to Eatonville, or somewhere similar. Oddly, he didn't have the urge to return to Seattle anymore.

The city was too far away from Danica.

No, he couldn't think like that. Rubbing his hand along the back of his neck, he reminded himself that she wasn't a part of his and Caden's future. On the other hand, it wasn't as if he'd spent a lot of time in Seattle. Not enough for it to feel like home.

Maybe he was just growing more accustomed to living the less hectic lifestyle of a small town. The recent attempts against him and Caden aside, it had been a nice place to live.

The hours passed by slowly, and he found himself wishing Hutch was there to help keep Caden entertained.

This full-time dad stuff was exhausting. It made him sympathize with what Annette had endured while he was overseas. Not that it justified her cheating, but he could see why being a mother without him to be there to help had been overwhelming.

It was close to dinnertime when Danica awoke.

"I feel so much better," she told the nurse who peered at her pupils. "Has there been any change in my neuro checks?"

"Your pupils are both equal now, which is great," the nurse said with a smile.

"Well, then, I'm sure I can be discharged tonight. Call the doctor—let him know I'd like to leave."

"Not until the morning." The nurse sounded calm, even though it was the second time she'd told Danica the same thing. "You don't want to underestimate a head injury."

"Yeah, yeah," she grumbled.

Colt and Sampson returned just then. "Hey, you're looking great, Danica."

"Thanks, but they still won't release me."

"That's for the best." Colt looked at him. "I'm ready to take you and Caden back to the lodge. Willow is still at the park."

"What did you and Willow find out about the blood at the Nisqually park entrance?" Danica asked.

"Looks to be the work of a poacher," Colt said. "Trent Ward, one of the park ranger techs, confirmed the blood wasn't human. It's from an elk. Willow is taking a look around, but it seems likely we'll hand the investigation over to the park rangers."

"Hunting isn't allowed in the park," Danica said with a frown. "No firearms are to be in there at all."

"Yeah, but the entrances aren't staffed, so there's no one to stop them." Colt turned toward him. "Ready to head back?"

He hesitated, glancing at Danica. "I had planned on staying here all night."

As if on cue, Caden began to fuss. Luke didn't want

to stay if there was any way Caden would prevent her from getting the rest she needed.

Danica reached over to take his hand. "Go back to the suite and get some sleep," she told him. "But I wouldn't mind being picked up in the morning." She frowned. "Early. I don't care what they say, I'm getting out of here first thing tomorrow."

"Okay, I'll take you up on that offer to head back to the lodge." He truly didn't want to leave but forced himself to do what was best for everyone. He turned to face Danica. "And I promise to be here bright and early to get you out of here."

"I'll hold you to that promise," she said in a mock threatening tone.

"Don't I know it," he teased. Luke pushed Caden from the room, following Colt and Sampson through the hospital. "Any sign of Alice Garth?"

"No. And I have to admit, it's strange." Colt glanced at him. "We'll find her, Luke."

The evening passed without a problem. Luke knew he and Caden were safe with Colt and Sampson, but it wasn't the same as sharing the space with Danica.

The following morning, Caden woke early. As he changed and fed the baby, Luke tried to get Caden to say *Da* again. The little boy was too focused on Sampson, repeating *doggy* over and over again.

"Hutch is going to be jealous at how much attention you're giving to Sampson," he told Caden.

"Doggy," Caden replied, hitting his rattle on the table.

They ate a quick breakfast and headed back outside. The dark, heavy clouds from the previous day had moved on, the sunshine a welcome change.

Luke pulled the car seat from Caden's stroller and placed him in Colt's SUV. He'd left his car at the hospital and looked forward to getting Danica and Hutch out of there.

"I can't understand why they haven't found Alice yet," he said as Colt navigated the highway toward Eatonville.

"The local police have had someone watching her house, but so far, she hasn't returned." Colt glanced at him. "I know it must be frustrating."

"You have no idea," Luke muttered, half under his breath. Granted, they were in the middle of the wilderness but it shouldn't be this difficult to find one woman.

To his surprise, at the hospital they found Danica dressed in her wrinkled uniform and more than ready to go.

"How's the headache?"

"Much better." She jumped up when they arrived. "I'm ready to get Hutch."

"I'm going to leave you both to it," Colt said. "Sampson and I are going to walk the area behind Alice Garth's house."

"Good plan," Danica agreed. "Colt, where's my SUV? Is it still parked near Alice Garth's house?"

"No, Willow and I moved it to the lodge parking lot," he admitted.

"We can use Luke's car then, even though it's not set up for Hutch," she said with a shrug.

"I can help," Colt offered. But seconds later, his radio crackled. He reached for it. "This is Officer Maxwell."

"A witness claims she saw the woman you're looking for. Can you get to Ashford to talk to her?"

"On it." Colt glanced at Danica. "Will you be okay?"

"I'm fine. I'm armed and I'll have Hutch soon, too. The veterinary clinic is only two blocks away and I need some fresh air. It will be quicker to walk back and forth, then use Luke's car to drive back to the lodge. Go find her, Colt."

"I'll be in touch," he said before rushing off.

Danica was given a package of discharge paperwork, with strict instructions to return immediately if any of her symptoms grew worse. She assured the nurse she would.

"I can't wait to have Hutch back," Danica confided as they made their way through the hospital to the main entrance. "That was the first night I was ever away from him."

"I'm sure he missed you, too." As they passed a job posting bulletin board, he slowed to read the various positions. There was one job for an emergency room technician, and he took a moment to consider that role as another potential opportunity. If the EMT position didn't work out, if the hours weren't conducive to caring for Caden, this was another possibility.

"You're interested in a job here?" Danica asked.

He lifted one shoulder. "Yeah, maybe. Depends on the hours. I need something reasonable to coincide with finding a daycare or babysitter for Caden."

"You must have decided against working in the hotel business with Eli Ballard."

"I'd rather put my medical skills to good use." He walked forward and held the door open for her. "Helping people one-on-one seems to be a better fit for me than running the lodge."

"Understandable." She winced and squinted in the bright sunshine. "I should have brought my sunglasses."

"We can stop to buy a pair," he offered. "Or I can grab my car."

"No need. It's closer to walk. Besides, I can't wait to see Hutch."

She quickened her pace, taking the sidewalk that would lead directly to the veterinary clinic.

He didn't mind the brisk pace, and Caden enjoyed it, too, waving his hands excitedly. It seemed Danica's headache was well under control, which was a relief. It felt good to be outside, with a hint of spring finally in the air.

Eatonville residents must have felt the same way, because many people were outside soaking up the sunshine. He noticed Danica swept her gaze over the area, as if expecting Alice Garth to pop up and make another attempt at Caden.

He looked around warily, too, but there was no sign of the woman resembling the driver's license photograph. He'd be on alert, even though he sincerely doubted Annette's mother would know to find them there.

"There's the clinic," Danica said excitedly.

"I remember." It seemed like months rather than a mere twenty-four hours ago since they'd brought Hutch here using a sheet as a sling.

Danica glanced up at him sheepishly. "I'm sure you think I'm overreacting."

"Not at all," he assured her. "Hutch is your partner. It's understandable that you miss him."

He didn't add that he missed having the large German shepherd hanging around, too. Probably as much as Caden did.

Upon reaching the clinic, he opened the door for her.

As Danica crossed the threshold, he heard a shout, followed by a wailing cry.

He turned to see who was hurt. A child was on the ground beside a toppled over bicycle. Even from here, he could see the girl's knee was bleeding.

Rather than following Danica inside, he turned to push Caden's stroller toward the injured girl. She was still wailing, and the boy next to her was shouting, too.

"That lady pushed her, did you see that? She pushed her right off the bike!"

Pushed? Luke frowned and pushed Caden's stroller faster. "Who did? What happened?"

"Look out!" A nanosecond after the kid shouted his warning, he sensed someone behind him. Luke instinctively turned, lifting his arm the same way he had outside the elevator lobby, instinctively sensing a blow was coming.

And it did. The bat connected with his shoulder, grazing the side of his head. He landed on the ground, pain reverberating through him as the stroller was wrenched from his hand.

Then he saw a woman wearing a long red coat, not black this time, running with surprising quickness while pushing Caden's stroller.

SIXTEEN

Danica had barely had a chance to reunite with Hutch when she heard someone shouting, "Look out!" Spinning toward the door, she belatedly realized Luke hadn't followed her inside the clinic. Then she gaped in horror when she saw a woman in a red coat strike Luke with a baseball bat, then wrench the stroller from his grip.

Not just any woman, but Vera. The lodge cook.

Vera was Alice! In a flash she remembered the strong scent of bleach from the kitchen when she was using Hutch to track the scent of the kidnapper. At the time she assumed the woman had been cleaning something, but now she understood Alice was smart enough to have used the bleach to mask her scent. She'd dyed her hair, maybe even gotten a perm to make it curly. Danica couldn't believe Vera was the person responsible, she'd crossed her off the list based on Greg's comment that she hadn't left the lodge the day of the kidnapping. She should have investigated her more closely.

She quickly unleashed her K-9 partner and pushed open the clinic door. "Get her, Hutch. Get Red!" She reached for her radio. "Colt, turn around. The kidnapper is here!"

Hutch bounded through the opening, sprinting after Alice. Danica ran, too, but Hutch was much quicker. She glanced toward Luke, worried that he needed medical care, but he'd managed to get to his feet to follow Alice, too.

Caden's grandmother had a head start, but Hutch was closing in. By now Luke had managed to stagger to his feet to join in the chase.

The edges of Alice's long red coat flapped as she ran, pushing the stroller. The underside of the coat was black. A reversible coat, she realized—just as Hutch lunged forward to grab it with his teeth.

"Let go!" Alice tried to grab the coat away from the dog, but Hutch didn't release her.

"Give it up, Alice or Vera, whatever you're calling yourself," Danica called as she worked hard to close the gap between them. "We know who you are. You're not getting away this time!"

The woman stumbled and once again tried to dislodge Hutch's grip on her coat, then she unzipped it and shrugged it off. The coat dropped to the ground and she began to run once again.

"Get her," Danica shouted again. Hutch dropped the coat, leaped over it and charged toward Alice. He was big and strong, and this time he clamped his mouth around her ankle, holding tight. The woman was so startled, she dropped the shortened baseball bat to the ground.

"Owwww," she shrieked. "Get him off! He's biting me!"

Alice's abrupt stop caused the stroller to rock back and forth precariously. The events in front of Danica seemed to unfold in slow motion. Hutch dug in his heels, holding Alice captive, while Luke was running full speed toward her from a perpendicular angle. The stroller slowly began to tip over, and Luke lunged forward in time to prevent Caden from hitting the ground.

"Let go!" Alice screamed louder now. "He's hurting me. I'll sue you for this!"

Danica would have laughed at the ridiculous threat if she'd had breath to spare. Instead, she pulled her cuffs from her belt and grabbed Alice's arm. Seconds later, she had the woman's wrists cuffed behind her back. She took a moment to look down at Hutch, "Good boy. Release, Hutch. Release."

Hutch let go of her ankle and sat, his tongue lolling to the side as if he'd enjoyed this recent romp to capture his quarry.

"Alice Garth, you're under arrest for kidnapping and assault on Luke and two police officers, including a K-9 officer. Did you kill Stacey and Jonas, too? Never mind, don't answer that. You have the right to remain silent. Anything you say can and will be used against you in a court of law. You have the right…"

"Caden is better off with me!" Alice loudly interrupted, glaring malevolently at Luke. "You're a terrible father, just like you were a terrible husband. I deserve Caden, don't you understand? I'll be his mother. I'll take care of him better than you ever could!"

Danica did her best to continue issuing the Miranda warning, but Caden's grandmother was clearly beyond reason. Thankfully, a couple of other officers had joined her and were able to witness her attempt to calm Alice down.

"Alice, I strongly suggest you exercise your right to remain silent," Danica repeated.

"After I learned your sister was murdered," she said without taking Danica's advice, "I knew it was the perfect time to get what I deserved. And no, I didn't kill your sister and her boyfriend. I only cared about my grandson. I figured I could take Caden and someone else would be blamed for kidnapping Caden, the same person who killed the others. Don't you see? Caden is mine! All mine!"

Luke unbuckled Caden from his stroller and cradled the little boy to his chest. "He's my son, not yours. But tell me this, Alice." He took a step closer, narrowing his gaze as he stared at her. "Why did Annette tell me you were dead? What kind of mother were you, that your own daughter claimed you died years ago? Huh? Tell me!"

Alice was flabbergasted by Luke's accusation, and her anger deflated as her tone turned whiney. "Annette had problems. You know that, Luke. You know she had problems—it's why your marriage didn't last. It's not my fault…"

"Enough." Danica was tired of listening to Alice's excuses. While Alice claimed she didn't kill Stacey and Jonas, she was guilty of plenty of other crimes. "This is your fault. Nothing excuses what you did. And now that you were kind enough to confess in front of so many witnesses—" Danica waved her arm at the crowd that had gathered around them. "You'll spend the rest of your life in prison."

"But—I didn't kill anyone… I missed my shot at Luke at the bridge—" Alice Garth glanced around the crowd and finally decided to shut up.

Danica turned toward the two local Eatonville cops who'd arrived on the scene. She hid a smile as they gave

Hutch a wide berth. "I need you to take her into custody. Hold her in your jail until I can arrange to have her transferred. Kidnapping is a federal offense, and I need to get in touch with my boss."

"Not a problem." The taller of the two officers stepped forward to take hold of Alice's arm. "This way, ma'am."

"Good boy, Hutch." Danica took the floppy-eared bunny from her pocket and tossed it up for him. He grabbed it and shook his head back and forth before running in a circle with the stuffed toy hanging half out of his mouth. Then she turned toward Luke. "Nice save with the stroller."

He bent to kiss Caden's head, then reached up to gingerly finger his temple. "I'm glad I could prevent Caden from falling. But she never should have gotten him in the first place. If not for that kid shouting a warning, I might have been knocked unconscious."

"I know, I heard him, too." She frowned. "It's your turn to be checked out at the hospital."

"Later." He dropped his hand. "She dyed her hair, made it curly and gained weight, or I would have recognized her sooner. But the eyes are Annette's. And she has the same widow's peak, too." He blew out a breath. "I think Alice pushed a girl off her bike to distract me. When the girl started crying and I could see that her knee was bleeding, I ran over to provide first aid."

"That's why you didn't follow me into the clinic." She sighed. "If I had known, I could have gone with you to check out the little girl."

"Well, as it turned out, Hutch was able to grab her." Luke looked fondly at her K-9 partner. "I'm impressed at how fast he is." His smile faded. "Alice never stood a chance."

"No, but Luke, knowing Vera is Alice makes me feel like a fool. Even with the hair dye and weight gain, I should have recognized her."

"There's no way you could have known," he countered. "She was so sweet to me and Caden. I never suspected her, especially since you were told she never left the lodge the day of the kidnapping."

"It's my job to keep everyone a suspect until proven otherwise." She raked a hand through her hair, hating that Vera had fooled her. Fooled them all, really, with her nice act. "Greg said she'd been in the lodge, but I should have dug deeper. The bleach smell from the kitchen should have been a huge red flag. But they do prepare food, and the place should be clean…"

"Don't beat yourself up, not after the way you and Hutch saved the day." Luke stared down at his son for a moment. "Do you think she's right?"

"Right? About what?"

"That I'm a lousy father?"

"No! Oh, Luke, absolutely not." Danica went over to wrap her arm around his shoulder. "You're a great father to Caden. She's the one who has issues, not you."

"I barely knew what I was doing when I first took over caring for him." Luke snaked his arm around her waist and pulled her close. "It's been a rough transition for the both of us, but we made it. Or I thought we had."

"You did, Luke. Caden adores you." She reached up to kiss his cheek, and at the same time, he turned his head toward her. Their mouths brushed, clung, then meshed.

Kissing Luke was amazing, but all too soon Caden

interrupted by patting Luke's chest to get his attention. "Dada."

She broke off the kiss and stared at Caden. "Did he really just say *dada*?"

"I—uh, think so." Luke's gaze lingered on her. "But I was too busy to notice."

She blushed, but before she could say anything more, she heard her name. "Danica! Are you okay?"

She turned in time to see Chief Fanelli striding toward her with four young men and women and their respective K-9s working hard to keep up with him. She moved away from Luke, hoping her boss hadn't seen their kiss.

The twinkle in Donovan's blue eyes squashed that hope. Her boss didn't miss much, and he'd obviously caught their kiss. She bent and put Hutch on leash to keep him under control around the strangers and the other dogs. "Hi, Donovan. I'm surprised to see you. What brings you here?"

"I decided to come in person to check up on you and Hutch. I take it seriously when two of my officers are injured in the line of duty." Donovan nodded at Luke, then turned back to face her. "I thought I'd catch you at the hospital, but you left early."

"Not that early," she protested, eyeing the four strangers and their German shepherds. Obviously, they were the new recruits for the PNK9 unit. Danica had been so busy she hadn't had a moment to even think about the candidates for the team's open slots. "Doc agreed I was stable for discharge."

"Hmm." Donovan eyed her thoughtfully, then smiled at Hutch, then Luke, too. "I heard you found and took down the kidnapper, although apparently she's not our murder suspect." He frowned slightly, then added, "Nice work, Danica."

"Thanks." She was all too conscious of the newcomers watching her.

"Danica, these are the four new recruits vying for our two open positions," Donovan said. "Sorry for the timing, but I'd like you to meet Desiree Eastwood and her K-9, Suvi, Parker Walsh and his K-9, Rosie, Brandie Weller and her K-9, Taz, and Owen Hannington with his K-9, Percy."

"Nice to meet all of you," Danica said with a smile.

"So, all this drama over catching a kidnapper, huh?" Parker said, looking unimpressed. "I've done that and more."

She lifted a brow as the two women rolled their eyes. She nodded at Desiree. "You're Jasmin's sister, aren't you?"

"Yes." Desiree shifted from one foot to the other, avoiding the gazes of her peers. "She told me how much she enjoys working with all of you as the team's tech expert."

"The feeling is mutual," Danica assured her.

"Glad you were able to solve this one," Owen said. He seemed the most easygoing of the bunch. Brandie didn't say anything, which she found curious. Maybe she was simply overwhelmed by the others she was competing against.

"Well, I wish you all the best," Danica said. She turned toward her boss. "I have some paperwork to finish up. I'll catch up with you and the others later. Alice claims she didn't kill anyone, and since she confessed to the kidnapping, I tend to believe her. We'll validate that, of course, but it looks as if we still have a double homicide to solve."

"We do, and we need to find the culprit sooner than later." Donovan frowned. "No matter where that investigation leads us."

She knew he meant Mara's possible involvement in the crime. Donovan turned away to address the new recruits. "I know you've been working on basic training, but I'm planning to split you up to work with my officers soon."

Danica watched them walk away, but then inwardly groaned when she saw Colt and Sampson swinging around them to come talk to her. "What's up, Colt?"

"Hey, sorry I didn't get here quicker." True regret flashed in his eyes. "If I'd have known the call was a false alarm, I'd have stayed."

"It's fine. We got the job done." She was anxious for him to move on so she could talk to Luke further. "Have fun with the new recruits."

"Yeah, thanks." He glanced over to where they stood around Donovan, then abruptly asked in a low voice, "Now that it seems Alice isn't the killer, do you think Mara's responsible for murdering Jonas and Stacey?"

Mara Gilmore was one of their own. She might have only been with the unit for a few months, but she was still PNK9.

"Honestly? I really don't know." She frowned. "I don't want to believe it, especially since the witness who claimed to see her shoot Stacey and Jonas is sketchy. But she ran away, Colt, and didn't answer the chief's call. Why would she do that? And she's nowhere to be found. She has to be in hiding."

"That's bothering me, too." He rubbed the back of his neck. "It's a tough situation."

"Yeah, and I'm worried it's going to mess with the camaraderie of our team. Willow and Mara's half brother, Asher, are obviously convinced she's innocent. From what I hear, people are taking sides, causing a rift among the team."

"We'll need to have faith that the truth will prevail." For a moment he looked so serious and intense, she knew he was thinking about something else. Likely his troubled past, but then it was gone. "I better get back to the newbies. I hope I'm not stuck with Parker—that guy seems too arrogant for his own good."

"Hey, if anyone can make him toe the line, it's you." She lightly bumped his shoulder with her fist. "Go get 'em."

Colt grinned and turned to lead Sampson back to the group. She watched them for a moment, then turned to find Luke placing Caden back in the stroller.

"I better take you back to your SUV," he said in a dull tone. "Sounds like you and Hutch are headed back to work."

The way he avoided her gaze made her frown. Was this it, then? Luke and Caden didn't need her protection any longer, but she didn't want to just walk away. And what about that kiss?

Was that Luke's way of saying goodbye?

His time with Danica and Hutch was over. Watching her with the team made him realize he wouldn't get to see her very often, if ever. Luke was grateful Alice Garth had been arrested, but letting Danica go was harder than he'd anticipated.

He loved her. In a way he'd never loved Annette. But it was all happening too soon, and he wasn't going to make that mistake again.

"This way. My car is in the hospital's parking lot, remember?" He pushed Caden's stroller in that direction.

"Luke, wait." She and Hutch picked up the pace to join him. "I know this has been a rough day."

That was putting it mildly. "To think Vera was Caden's grandmother this whole time..."

"I know." She lightly touched his arm, and it was all he could do not to pull her back into his arms. "We'll need to talk to Eli right away. He'll have to find a new cook."

"If he hasn't figured that out already." He glanced at her. "Vera—I mean, Alice—showing up here in Eatonville to kidnap Caden means she's not working the kitchen."

"True." She shook her head. "She must have realized I'd be brought here and that I'd pick up Hutch this morning. For all her wild talk, she's a smart lady. Yet I'm still having trouble connecting that sweet, doting woman to the one who shot at you, hit Hutch with a tranquilizer gun and used that shortened bat against both of us just to get what she wanted."

"She won't hurt anyone ever again." Luke drummed up a smile. "Thanks to you."

"And you," she insisted. When they reached his car, she turned to face him. "Luke, I know you and Caden don't need protection anymore, but I'm curious about your plans moving forward. Are you still thinking of applying for a job in the medical field?"

"Yes. I don't want to run the lodges, and since Eli Ballard asked that we keep lines of communication open, I'm going to let him know of my intent to sell. Well, once Stacey's estate is settled, that is. Not so much for the money, because I'm doing okay, but because this way Eli can look into buying me out and we'll go from there."

She nodded slowly, then said, "I want to see you again. And Caden, too."

He stared at her for a moment. "You do?"

"Yes. I—uh, well, you know how I grew up, landing in foster care after testifying against my dad for killing my mother. I never planned on having a family, but being with you these past few days has made me realize just what I've been missing." She flushed, then said, "I know you're not interested in getting serious with anyone, either, but maybe we can hang out, you know, as friends."

"Friends." The corner of his mouth twitched. "Oh, I think we can do better than that."

"We can?" Confusion clouded her light brown eyes.

"Yeah." He gently pulled her into his arms, holding her close in a way he hadn't been able to do earlier with Caden tucked against him. "I care about you, Danica. More than I thought possible."

"Oh," she murmured breathlessly moments before he captured her lips in a deep kiss. He took his time exploring her mouth, relieved when there were no more interruptions.

He would have stood there kissing her forever, but of course, with a baby that wasn't possible. Hutch was his usual well trained self, but Caden began to smack his rattle on the edge of the stroller.

"Daddy!"

After all this time, his son had learned how to say

Daddy. It made him smile, even though his son's timing couldn't be worse. He reluctantly broke off from kissing Danica, rested his forehead against hers for a moment, then said, "I think I've fallen in love with you."

"Wait. You what?" Danica's jaw dropped in a way that made him want to kiss her again.

"I love you." The more he said the words, the more he knew they were true. There was none of the panic he'd experienced when he'd hastily married Annette. He knew her well enough to know Danica would never cheat or lie. "I've been fighting my feelings because I don't want to make the same mistake I had with Annette. We rushed into marriage, and family, despite knowing I had another two years left to serve in the army." He tucked a strand of hair behind her ear. "But I think you should know I'm serious about spending time with you. In seeing how we can make a relationship between us work." He hesitated, then added, "If you'll give me a chance."

"Yes, Luke. I'll give you a chance, because I think I've fallen in love with you, too." Tears glistened in her eyes. "I've loved spending time with you and didn't want to leave. But I don't know much about being in a relationship, so try to be patient with me. I'm sure I'll make mistakes."

"We'll both make mistakes, but as long as we love each other and remain open and honest about our feelings, we'll find a way to work things out." It was what he should have done with Annette. Not that he could help being deployed, but still. He'd known she wasn't happy.

Now that he'd met her mother, he understood there was a lot he hadn't known about the woman he'd married. And he doubted he'd ever truly know about Annette's dysfunctional relationship with her mother. There must be some reason she'd told him Alice was dead. So many secrets and lies.

Yet Danica had been up-front and honest about her past life, bluntly telling him everything she'd gone through. He loved and admired her, not just for being honest, but for how she'd triumphed over her painful past.

"I believe God brought us together for a reason," she said. "And I'm so grateful for His blessing."

"Me, too." He imagined Stacey smiling down at them from Heaven as he hugged her again. Then he stepped back. "Come on, we should get back. You mentioned something about paperwork."

"I can do that online." She opened the back door to let Hutch in. He didn't have a crated area for the K-9, but that was something he'd consider down the road. "I think we should stop for something to eat, though. Can't depend on having anything at the lodge."

He chuckled and nodded. As he disassembled the stroller and buckled Caden into the back seat under Hutch's watchful eye, a wave of hope combined with sheer happiness washed over him.

It was early in their burgeoning relationship, especially since Danica and her team still had a murder to solve, but he knew Danica and Hutch would someday soon be his new family.

And he couldn't imagine a better gift from God.

* * * * *

Dear Reader,

I hope you enjoyed Shielding the Baby, the first book in the new Pacific Northwest K-9 Unit series! I'm blessed the editorial staff at Love Inspired Suspense continue to create the framework for these great stories and that I'm able to participate. Without our wonderful editor, Emily Rodmell, these books wouldn't be possible. I am also thankful to work with an outstanding group of authors. You won't want to miss a single book in this series.

I adore hearing from my readers! I can be found through my website at https://www.laurascottbooks.com, via Facebook at https://www.facebook.com/LauraScottBooks, on Instagram at https://www.instagram.com/laurascottbooks/ and on Twitter https://twitter.com/laurascottbooks. Also, take a moment to sign up for my monthly newsletter, to learn about my new book releases! All subscribers receive a free novella not available for purchase on any platform.

Until next time,
Laura Scott

Get 4 FREE REWARDS!

We'll send you 2 FREE Books plus 2 FREE Mystery Gifts.

FREE
Value Over
$20

Both the **Love Inspired®** and **Love Inspired® Suspense** series feature compelling novels filled with inspirational romance, faith, forgiveness and hope.

HARLEQUIN
PLUS

Try the best multimedia subscription service for romance readers like you!

Read, Watch and Play.

Experience the easiest way to get the romance content you crave.

Start your **FREE TRIAL** at
<u>www.harlequinplus.com/freetrial</u>.